BORÍS GODUNÓV

BORÍS · GODUNÓV
A DRAMA IN VERSE

By
Alexander Sergyeyevich Pushkin

Rendered into English Verse by
ALFRED HAYES

With Preface by
C. NABOKOFF
(Minister Plenipotentiary in England)

SECOND IMPRESSION

LONDON
KEGAN PAUL, TRENCH, TRÜBNER & CO. LTD.

P. DUTTON AND COMPANY, INC.
NEW YORK

PREFACE

By C. Nabokoff

THE average educated Russian is intensely fond of poetry, literature, and music. Everyone has his favourite poet, writer, or musician, but there is one poet whose immeasurable superiority over all others is universally acknowledged in Russia. That poet is Alexander Pushkin ; most Russians believe that Pushkin is the greatest poet that ever lived. We not only admire him, we worship him ; he stands apart. There is no other poet as versatile as Pushkin—lyrics, epic, satire, novels, historical drama, ballads, fairy tales in verse, he has left masterpieces in every one of these forms of art, so we believe. And of all he has written, with the one possible exception of his romance in verse, *Evgueni Onieguine*, the drama *Borís Godunóv* is thought to be his greatest work.

Pushkin, an exile living on his estate near Pskof, read the *History of Russia* by our first great historian Karamzin, and was particularly interested in the period of Russian history which preceded the so-called ' Troubled Times ' the first decade of the seventeenth century. This period offers indeed ample material for historical drama or chronicle. Pushkin's desire to dramatise the narrative of Karamzin was further stimulated by the study of Shakespeare, whose tragedies he undoubtedly accepted as a model. The influence of Shakespeare on Pushkin's work was so far-reaching that it deserves a special study which is, however, outside the scope of these remarks.

Borís Godunóv, in inspiration, in its general structure, in the masterful intuition of historical atmosphere, so closely resembles Shakespeare's great tragedies that one is almost tempted to describe this drama as an adaptation of Shakespeare to Russian history. This resemblance never appeared so striking to me as when I read Mr Hayes' translation, in itself a work of the loftiest kind. I confess that when I first received Mr Hayes' manuscript, I was not free from misgivings. There are certain passages in *Borís Godunóv*, namely, the scene in Pimen's cell, the dialogue between the Pretender and Marina, known as the 'Scene by the Fountain,' and the monologue of Borís, 'I have attained supreme power,' which Russians have always considered untranslatable and the music of the Russian language in these scenes impossible to render in any other language. Mr Hayes has achieved the impossible.

I have no doubt that the reader who is not acquainted with the original will appreciate the beauty of Mr Hayes' inspiration ; for myself, I can pay no higher tribute to his achievement than by saying that the translation is worthy of the original.

The scenic production of *Borís Godunóv* is an extremely difficult task, as no less than twenty-four changes of scenery are required if the drama is to be produced as it is written. A revolving stage alone affords this possibility. *Borís* is not, therefore, a ' pièce du répertoire ' in Russia, and an effort of even greater magnitude would be necessary for the production in England. Nevertheless, it is to be hoped that Mr Hayes' remarkable translation will gain wide popularity in this country. For the last three years much has been done to promote the study of Russian art and literature in Great Britain and to spread the knowledge of the Russian language. Mr Hayes' translation of *Borís Godunóv* will undoubtedly be of much value to teachers of Russian in England.

C. NABOKOFF

PREFATORY NOTE

THE thanks of the translator are due to Dr Louis Segal for his valuable help in the revision of this work, and to Professor Granville Bantock at whose suggestion it was undertaken.

A. H.

DRAMATIS PERSONÆ*

BORÍS GODUNÓV, *afterwards Tsar.*

PRINCE SHUISKY
PRINCE VOROTINSKY } *Russian nobles.*

SHCHELKÁLOV, *Russian Minister of State.*

FATHER PIMEN, *an old monk and chronicler.*

GREGORY OTRÉPIEV, *a young monk, afterwards the Pretender to the throne of Russia.*

THE PATRIARCH.   ABBOT OF THE CHUDOV MONASTERY.

MISSAIL
VARLAAM } *wandering friars.*

ATHANASIUS MIKAILOVICH PÚSHKIN, *friend of Prince Shuisky.*

FEÓDOR, *young son of Borís Godunóv.*

SEMYÓN NIKITICH GODUNÓV, *secret agent of Borís Godunóv.*

GABRIEL PÚSHKIN, *nephew of A. M. Púshkin.*

PRINCE KÚRBSKY
KHRUSHCHOV } *disgraced Russian nobles.*

KARÉLA, *a Cossack.*

PRINCE VISHNEVETSKY.   MNÍSHEK, *Governor of Sambór.*

BASMÁNOV, *a Russian officer.*

MARZHERET
ROZEN } *officers of the Pretender.*

DIMÍTRY, *the Pretender, formerly Gregory Otrépiev.*

MOSALSKY, *a Boyár.*

KSENIA, *daughter of Borís Godunóv.*   NURSE *of Ksenia.*

MARINA, *daughter of Mníshek.*

ROUZYA, *tire-woman of Ksenia.*   HOSTESS *of tavern.*

Boyárs, The People, Inspectors, Officers, Attendants, Guests, a Boy in attendance on Prince Shuisky, a Catholic Priest, a Polish Noble, a Poet, an Idiot, a Beggar, Gentlemen, Peasants, Guards, Russian, Polish, and German Soldiers, a Russian Prisoner of War, Boys, an old Woman, Ladies, Serving-women.

---

* The list of *Dramatis Personæ* which does not appear in the original has been added for the convenience of the reader —A.H.

BORÍS GODUNÓV

(1825)

PALACE OF THE KREMLIN

(FEBRUARY 20TH, A.D. 1598)

PRINCE SHUISKY and VOROTÍNSKY

VOROTÍNSKY. To keep the city's peace, that is the task
    Entrusted to us twain, but you forsooth
    Have little need to watch ; Moscow is empty ;
    The people to the Monastery have flocked
    After the patriarch.   What thinkest thou ?
    How will this trouble end ?

SHUISKY.   How will it end ?
    That is not hard to tell.   A little more
    The multitude will groan and wail, Borís
    Pucker awhile his forehead, like a toper
    Eyeing a glass of wine, and in the end
    Will humbly of his graciousness consent
    To take the crown ; and then --and then will rule us
    Just as before.

VOROTÍNSKY.   A month has flown already
Since, cloistered with his sister, he forsook
The world's affairs.   None hitherto hath shaken
His purpose, not the patriarch, not the boyárs
His counsellors ; their tears, their prayers he heeds not ;
Deaf is he to the wail of Moscow, deaf
To the Great Council's voice ; vainly they urged
The sorrowful nun-queen to consecrate
Borís to sovereignty ; firm was his sister,
Inexorable as he ; methinks Borís
Inspired her with this spirit.   What if our ruler
Be sick in very deed of cares of state
And hath no strength to mount the throne ?   What
     say'st thou ?

SHUISKY.   I say that in that case the blood in vain
Flowed of the young tsarévich, that Dimítry
Might just as well be living.

VOROTÍNSKY.   Fearful crime !
Is it beyond all doubt Borís contrived
The young boy's murder ?

SHUISKY.   Who besides ?   Who else
Bribed Chepchugóv in vain ?   Who sent in secret
The brothers Bityagóvsky with Kachálov ?

Myself was sent to Úglich, there to probe
This matter on the spot ; fresh traces there
I found ; the whole town bore witness to the crime ;
With one accord the burghers all affirmed it ;
And with a single word, when I returned,
I could have proved the secret villain's guilt.

VOROTÍNSKY. Why didst thou then not crush him ?

SHUISKY.   At the time,
I do confess, his unexpected calmness,
His shamelessness, dismayed me. Honestly
He looked me in the eyes ; he questioned me
Closely, and I repeated to his face
The foolish tale himself had whispered to me.

VOROTÍNSKY. An ugly business, prince.

SHUISKY.   What could I do ?
Declare all to Feódor ? But the tsar
Saw all things with the eyes of Godunóv,
Heard all things with the ears of Godunóv ;
Grant even that I might have fully proved it,
Borís would have denied it there and then,
And I should have been haled away to prison,
And in good time—like mine own uncle—strangled

Within the silence of some deaf-walled dungeon.
I boast not when I say that, given occasion,
No penalty affrights me.   I am no coward,
But also am no fool, and do not choose
Of my free will to walk into a halter.

VOROTÍNSKY.   Monstrous misdeed !   Listen ; I warrant you
Remorse already gnaws the murderer ;
Be sure the blood of that same innocent child
Will hinder him from mounting to the throne.

SHUISKY.   That will not baulk him ; Borís is not so timid !
What honour for ourselves, ay, for all Russia !
A slave of yesterday, a Tartar, son
By marriage of Maliúta, of a hangman,
Himself in soul a hangman, he to wear
The crown and robe of Monomakh !——

VOROTÍNSKY.   You are right ;
He is of lowly birth ; we twain can boast
A nobler lineage.

SHUISKY.   Indeed we may !

VOROTÍNSKY.   Let us remember, Shuisky, Vorotínsky
Are, let me say, born princes.

SHUISKY. Yea, born princes,
And of the blood of Rurik.

VOROTÍNSKY. Listen, prince;
Then we, 'twould seem, should have the right to mount
Feódor's throne.

SHUISKY. Rather than Godunóv.

VOROTÍNSKY. In very truth 'twould seem so.

SHUISKY. And what then ?
If still Borís pursue his crafty ways,
Let us contrive by skilful means to rouse
The people. Let them turn from Godunóv ;
Princes they have in plenty of their own ;
Let them from out their number choose a tsar.

VOROTÍNSKY. Of us, Varyágs in blood, there are full many,
But 'tis no easy thing for us to vie
With Godunóv ; the people are not wont
To recognise in us an ancient branch
Of their old warlike masters ; long already
Have we our appanages forfeited,
Long served but as lieutenants of the tsars,
And he hath known, by fear, and love, and glory,
How to bewitch the people.

SHUISKY. (*Looking through a window.*) He has dared,
That's all—while we— Enough of this.   Thou seest
Dispersedly the people are returning.
We'll go forthwith and learn what is resolved.

THE RED SQUARE

THE PEOPLE

1ST PERSON.   He is inexorable !   He thrust from him
Prelates, boyárs, and Patriarch ; in vain
Prostrate they fall ; the splendour of the throne
Affrights him.

2ND PERSON.   O, my God, who is to rule us ?
O, woe to us !

3RD PERSON.   See ! the Chief Minister
Is coming out to tell us what the Council
Has now resolved.

THE PEOPLE.   Silence !   Silence !   He speaks,
The Minister of State.   Hush, hush !   Give ear !

SHCHELKÁLOV.   (*From the Red Balcony.*)
The Council have resolved for the last time
To put to proof the power of supplication
Upon our ruler's mournful soul.   At dawn,
After a solemn service in the Kremlin,
The blessèd Patriarch will go, preceded

By sacred banners, with the holy ikons
Of Donsky and Vladímir ; with him go
The Council, courtiers, delegates, boyárs,
And all the orthodox folk of Moscow ; all
Will go to pray once more the queen to pity
Fatherless Moscow, and to consecrate
Borís unto the crown.   Now to your homes
Go ye in peace : pray ; and to Heaven shall rise
The heart's petition of the orthodox.

(*The* PEOPLE *disperse.*)

THE VIRGIN'S FIELD

THE NEW NUNNERY. The People.

1st Person. To plead with the tsarítsa in her cell
Now are they gone. Thither have gone Borís,
The Patriarch, and a host of boyárs.

2nd Person. What news ?

3rd Person. Still is he obdurate ; yet there is hope.

Peasant Woman. (*With a child.*)
Drat you ! stop crying, or else the bogie-man
Will carry you off. Drat you, drat you ! stop crying !

1st Person. Can't we slip through behind the fence ?

2nd Person. Impossible !
No chance at all ! Not only is the nunnery
Crowded ; the precincts too are crammed with people.
Look what a sight ! All Moscow has thronged here.
See ! fences, roofs, and every single storey
Of the Cathedral bell tower, the church-domes,
The very crosses are studded thick with people.

B

1ST PERSON.   A goodly sight indeed !

2ND PERSON.   What is that noise ?

3RD PERSON.   Listen !   What noise is that ?—The people
      groaned ;
      See there !   They fall like waves, row upon row—
      Again—again— Now, brother, 'tis our turn ;
      Be quick, down on your knees !

THE PEOPLE.   (*On their knees, groaning and wailing.*)
                                   Have pity on us,
      Our father !   O, rule over us !   O, be
      Father to us, and tsar !

1ST PERSON.   (*Sotto voce.*)   Why are they wailing ?

2ND PERSON.   How can we know ?   The boyárs know well
      enough.
      It's not our business.

PEASANT WOMAN.   (*With child.*)
                                   Now, what's this ?   Just when
      It ought to cry, the child stops crying.   I'll show you !
      Here comes the bogie-man !   Cry, cry, you spoilt one !
            (*Throws it on the ground ; the child screams.*)
      That's right, that's right !

1ST PERSON.   As everyone is crying,
     We also, brother, will begin to cry.

2ND PERSON.   Brother, I try my best, but can't.

1ST PERSON.   Nor I.
     Have you not got an onion ?

2ND PERSON.   No ; I'll wet
     My eyes with spittle.   What's up there now ?

1ST PERSON.   Who knows
     What's going on ?

THE PEOPLE.   The crown for him !   He is tsar !
     He has yielded !—Borís !—our tsar !—Long live Borís !

THE PALACE OF THE KREMLIN

BORÍS, PATRIARCH, Boyárs

BORÍS. Thou, father Patriarch, all ye boyárs !
My soul lies bare before you ; ye have seen
With what humility and fear I took
This mighty power upon me.   Ah ! how heavy
My weight of obligation !   I succeed
The great Iváns ; succeed the angel tsar !—
O Righteous Father, King of kings, look down
From Heaven upon the tears of Thy true servants,
And send on him whom Thou hast loved, whom Thou
Exalted hast on earth so wondrously,
Thy holy blessing.   May I rule my people
In glory, and like Thee be good and righteous !
To you, boyárs, I look for help.   Serve me
As ye served him, what time I shared your labours,
Ere I was chosen by the people's will.

BOYÁRS.   We will not from our plighted oath depart.

BORÍS.   Now let us go to kneel before the tombs
Of Russia's great departed rulers.   Then
Bid summon all our people to a feast,

All, from the noble to the poor blind beggar.
To all free entrance, all most welcome guests.

(*Exit, the* BOYÁRS *following.*)

PRINCE VOROTÍNSKY. (*Stopping Shuisky.*)
You rightly guessed.

SHUISKY. Guessed what ?

VOROTÍNSKY. Why, you remember—
The other day, here on this very spot.

SHUISKY. No, I remember nothing.

VOROTÍNSKY. When the people
Flocked to the Virgin's Field, thou said'st——

SHUISKY. 'Tis not
The time for recollection. There are times
When I should counsel you not to remember,
But even to forget. And for the rest,
I sought but by feigned calumny to prove thee,
The truelier to discern thy secret thoughts.
But see ! the people hail the tsar—my absence
May be remarked. I'll join them.

VOROTÍNSKY. Wily courtier !

NIGHT

Cell in the Monastery of Chudov (A.D. 1603)

FATHER PIMEN, GREGORY (sleeping)

PIMEN (*Writing in front of a sacred lamp.*)
One more, the final record, and my annals
Are ended, and fulfilled the duty laid
By God on me a sinner.   Not in vain
Hath God appointed me for many years
A witness, teaching me the art of letters ;
A day will come when some laborious monk
Will bring to light my zealous, nameless toil,
Kindle, as I, his lamp, and from the parchment
Shaking the dust of ages will transcribe
My true narrations, that posterity
The bygone fortunes of the orthodox
Of their own land may learn, will mention make
Of their great tsars, their labours, glory, goodness—
And humbly for their sins, their evil deeds,
Implore the Saviour's mercy.—In old age
I live anew ; the past unrolls before me.—
Did it in years long vanished sweep along,
Full of events, and troubled like the deep ?

Now it is hushed and tranquil. Few the faces
Which memory hath saved for me, and few
The words which have come down to me ;—the rest
Have perished, never to return.—But day
Draws near, the lamp burns low, one record more,
The last. (*He writes.*)

GREGORY. (*Waking.*) Ever the selfsame dream! Is 't
  possible ?

For the third time ! Accursèd dream ! And ever
Before the lamp sits the old man and writes—
And not all night, 'twould seem, from drowsiness,
Hath closed his eyes. I love the peaceful sight,
When, with his soul deep in the past immersed,
He keeps his chronicle. Oft have I longed
To guess what 'tis he writes of. Is 't perchance
The dark dominion of the Tartars ? Is it
Iván's grim punishments, the stormy Council
Of Nóvgorod ? Is it about the glory
Of our dear fatherland ?—I ask in vain !
Not on his lofty brow, nor in his looks
May one peruse his secret thoughts ; always
The same aspect ; lowly at once, and lofty—
Like some state Minister grown grey in office,
Calmly alike he contemplates the just
And guilty, with indifference he hears
Evil and good, and knows not wrath nor pity.

PIMEN.   Wakest thou, brother ?

GREGORY.   Honoured father, give me
Thy blessing.

PIMEN.   May God bless thee on this day,
To-morrow, and for ever.

GREGORY.   All night long
Thou hast been writing and abstained from sleep,
While demon visions have disturbed my peace,
The fiend molested me.   I dreamed I scaled
By winding stairs a turret, from whose height
Moscow appeared an anthill, where the people
Seethed in the squares below and pointed at me
With laughter.   Shame and terror came upon me—
And falling headlong, I awoke.   Three times
I dreamed the selfsame dream.   Is it not strange ?

PIMEN.   'Tis the young blood at play ; humble thyself
By prayer and fasting, and thy slumber's visions
Will all be filled with lightness.   Hitherto
If I, unwillingly by drowsiness
Weakened, make not at night long orisons,
My old-man's sleep is neither calm nor sinless ;
Now riotous feasts appear, now camps of war,
Scuffles of battle, fatuous diversions
Of youthful years.

GREGORY. How joyfully didst thou
Live out thy youth ! The fortress of Kazán
Thou fought'st beneath, with Shuisky didst repulse
The army of Litvá. Thou hast seen the court,
And splendour of Iván. Ah ! happy thou !
Whilst I, from boyhood up, a wretched monk,
Wander from cell to cell ! Why unto me
Was it not given to play the game of war,
To revel at the table of a tsar ?
Then, like to thee, would I in my old age
Have gladly from the noisy world withdrawn,
To vow myself a dedicated monk,
And in the quiet cloister end my days.

PIMEN. Complain not, brother, that the sinful world
Thou early didst forsake, that few temptations
The All-Highest sent to thee. Believe my words ;
The glory of the world, its luxury,
Woman's seductive love, seen from afar,
Enslave our souls. Long have I lived, have taken
Delight in many things, but never knew
True bliss until that season when the Lord
Guided me to the cloister. Think, my son,
On the great tsars ; who loftier than they ?
God only. Who dares thwart them ? None. What
then ?

Often the golden crown became to them
A burden ; for a cowl they bartered it.
The tsar Iván sought in monastic toil
Tranquillity ; his palace, filled erewhile
With haughty minions, grew to all appearance
A monastery ; the very rakehells seemed
Obedient monks, the terrible tsar appeared
A pious abbot.   Here, in this very cell
(At that time Cyril, the much suffering,
A righteous man, dwelt in it ; even me
God then made comprehend the nothingness
Of worldly vanities), here I beheld,
Weary of angry thoughts and executions,
The tsar ; among us, meditative, quiet
Here sat the Terrible ; we motionless
Stood in his presence, while he talked with us
In tranquil tones.   Thus spake he to the abbot
And all the brothers : " My fathers, soon will come
The longed-for day ; here shall I stand before you,
Hungering for salvation ; Nicodemus
Thou Sergius, Cyril thou, will all accept
My spiritual vow ; to you I soon shall come
Accurst in sin, here the clean habit take,
Prostrate, most holy father, at thy feet."
So spake the sovereign lord, and from his lips

Sweetly the accents flowed.   He wept ; and we
With tears prayed God to send His love and peace
Upon his suffering and stormy soul.—
What of his son Feódor ?   On the throne
He sighed to lead the life of calm devotion.
The royal chambers to a cell of prayer
He turned, wherein the heavy cares of state
Vexed not his holy soul.   God grew to love
The tsar's humility ; in his good days
Russia was blest with glory undisturbed,
And in the hour of his decease was wrought
A miracle unheard of ; at his bedside,
Seen by the tsar alone, appeared a being
Exceeding bright, with whom Feódor 'gan
To commune, calling him great Patriarch ;—
And all around him were possessed with fear,
Musing upon the vision sent from Heaven,
Since at that time the Patriarch was not present
In church before the tsar.   And when he died
The palace was with holy fragrance filled,
And like the sun his countenance outshone.
Never again shall we see such a tsar.—
O, horrible, appalling woe !   We have sinned,
We have angered God ; we have chosen for our ruler
A tsar's assassin.

GREGORY.   Honoured father, long
   Have I desired to ask thee of the death
   Of young Dimítry, the tsarévich ; thou,
   'Tis said, wast then at Úglich.

PIMEN.   Ay, my son,
   I well remember. God it was who led me
   To witness that ill deed, that bloody sin.
   I at that time was sent to distant Úglich
   Upon some mission. I arrived at night.
   Next morning, at the hour of holy mass,
   I heard upon a sudden a bell toll ;
   'Twas the alarm bell. Then a cry, an uproar ;
   Men rushing to the court of the tsarítsa.
   Thither I haste, and there had flocked already
   All Úglich. There I see the young tsarévich
   Lie slaughtered : the queen mother in a swoon
   Bowed over him, his nurse in her despair
   Wailing ; and then the maddened people drag
   The godless, treacherous nurse away. Appears
   Suddenly in their midst, wild, pale with rage,
   Judas Bityágovsky. " There, there's the villain ! "
   Shout on all sides the crowd, and in a trice
   He was no more. Straightway the people rushed
   On the three fleeing murderers ; they seized
   The hiding miscreants and led them up
   To the child's corpse yet warm ; when lo ! a marvel—

The dead child all at once began to tremble !
" Confess ! " the people thundered ; and in terror
Beneath the axe the villains did confess—
And named Borís.

GREGORY.   How many summers lived
The murdered boy ?

PIMEN.   Seven summers ; he would now
(Since then have passed ten years—nay, more—twelve
   years)
He would have been of equal age to thee,
And would have reigned ; but God deemed otherwise.
This is the lamentable tale wherewith
My chronicle doth end ; since then I little
Have dipped in worldly business. Brother Gregory,
Thou hast illumed thy mind by earnest study ;
To thee I hand my task. In hours exempt
From the soul's exercise, do thou record,
Not subtly reasoning, all things whereto
Thou shalt in life be witness ; war and peace,
The sway of kings, the holy miracles
Of saints, all prophecies and heavenly signs ;—
For me 'tis time to rest and quench my lamp.—
But hark ! the matin bell. Bless, Lord, Thy servants !
Give me my crutch.

                                   (*Exit.*)

GREGORY.   Borís, Borís, before thee
   All tremble ; none dares even to remind thee
   Of what befell the hapless child ; meanwhile
   Here in dark cell a hermit doth indite
   Thy stern denunciation. Thou wilt not
   Escape the judgment even of this world,
   As thou wilt not escape the doom of God.

FENCE OF THE MONASTERY *

GREGORY and a Wicked Monk

GREGORY.   O, what a weariness is our poor life,
What misery !   Day comes, day goes, and ever
Is seen, is heard one thing alone ; one sees
Only black cassocks, only hears the bell.
Yawning by day you wander, wander, nothing
To do ; you doze ; the whole night long till daylight
The poor monk lies awake ; and when in sleep
You lose yourself, black dreams disturb the soul ;
Glad that they sound the bell, that with a crutch
They rouse you.   No, I will not suffer it !
I cannot !   Through this fence I'll flee !   The world
Is great ; my path is on the highways   never
Thou'lt hear of me again.

MONK.   Truly your life
Is but a sorry one, ye dissolute,
Wicked young monks !

---

* This scene was omitted by Púshkin from the published version of
the play.

GREGORY. Would that the Khan again
Would come upon us, or Lithuania rise
Once more in insurrection. Good! I would then
Cross swords with them! Or what if the tsarévich
Should suddenly arise from out the grave,
Should cry, " Where are ye, children, faithful servants?
Help me against Borís, against my murderer!
Seize my foe, lead him to me! "

MONK. Enough, my friend,
Of empty babble. We cannot raise the dead.
No, clearly it was fated otherwise
For the tsarévich— But hearken; if you wish
To do a thing, then do it.

GREGORY. What to do?

MONK. If I were young as thou, if these grey hairs
Had not already streaked my beard— Dost take me?

GREGORY. Not I.

MONK. Hearken; our folk are dull of brain,
Easy of faith, and glad to be amazed
By miracles and novelties. The boyárs
Remember Godunóv as erst he was,

Peer to themselves; and even now the race
Of the old Varyágs is loved by all. Thy years
Match those of the tsarévich. If thou hast
Cunning and hardihood— Dost take me now ?

GREGORY. I take thee.

MONK. Well, what say'st thou ?

GREGORY. 'Tis resolved :
I am Dimítry, I tsarévich !

MONK. Give me
Thy hand, my bold young friend. Thou shalt be tsar !

PALACE OF THE PATRIARCH

PATRIARCH, ABBOT of the Chudov Monastery

PATRIARCH. And he has run away, Father Abbot?

ABBOT. He has run away, holy sovereign, now three days ago.

PATRIARCH. Accursèd rascal! What is his origin?

ABBOT. Of the family of the Otrépievs, of the lower nobility of Galicia; in his youth he took the tonsure, no one knows where, lived at Suzdal, in the Ephimievsky monastery, departed from there, wandered to various convents, finally arrived at my Chudov fraternity; but I, seeing that he was still young and inexperienced, entrusted him at the outset to Father Pimen, an old man, kind and humble. And he was very learned, read our chronicle, composed canons for the holy brethren; but, to be sure, instruction was not given to him from the Lord God——

PATRIARCH. Ah, those learned fellows! What a thing to say, " I shall be tsar in Moscow." Ah, he is a vessel of

the devil! However, it is no use even to report to the
tsar about this; why disquiet our father sovereign?
It will be enough to give information about his flight to
the Secretary Smirnov or the Secretary Ephimiev.
What a heresy: "I shall be tsar in Moscow!" . . .
Catch, catch the fawning villain, and send him to
Solovetsky to perpetual penance. But this—is it not
heresy, Father Abbot?

ABBOT. Heresy, holy Patriarch; downright heresy.

PALACE OF THE TSAR

Two Attendants

1st ATTENDANT.   Where is the sovereign ?

2nd ATTENDANT.   In his bed-chamber,
Where he is closeted with some magician.

1st ATTENDANT.   Ay ; that's the kind of intercourse he
    loves ;
Sorcerers, fortune-tellers, necromancers.
Ever he seeks to dip into the future,
Just like some pretty girl.   Fain would I know
What 'tis he would foretell.

2nd ATTENDANT.   Well, here he comes.
Will it please you question him ?

1st ATTENDANT.   How grim he looks !
                                    (*Exeunt.*)

TSAR.   (*Enters.*) I have attained the highest power. Six
    years
Already have I reigned in peace ; but joy

Dwells not within my soul.   Even so in youth
We greedily desire the joys of love,
But only quell the hunger of the heart
With momentary possession.   We grow cold,
Grow weary and oppressed !   In vain the wizards
Promise me length of days, days of dominion
Immune from treachery—not power, not life
Gladden me ; I forebode the wrath of Heaven
And woe.   For me no happiness.   I thought
To satisfy my people in contentment,
In glory, gain their love by generous gifts,
But I have put away that empty hope ;
The power that lives is hateful to the mob,—
Only the dead they love.   We are but fools
When our heart vibrates to the people's groans
And passionate wailing.   Lately on our land
God sent a famine ; perishing in torments
The people uttered moan.   The granaries
I made them free of, scattered gold among them,
Found labour for them ; furious for my pains
They cursed me !   Next, a fire consumed their homes ;
I built for them new dwellings ; then forsooth
They blamed me for the fire !   Such is the mob,
Such is its judgment !   Seek its love, indeed !
I thought within my family to find
Solace ; I thought to make my daughter happy

By wedlock. Like a tempest Death took off
Her bridegroom—and at once a stealthy rumour
Pronounced me guilty of my daughter's grief—
Me, me, the hapless father! Whoso dies,
I am the secret murderer of all ;
I hastened Feódor's end, 'twas I that poisoned
My sister-queen, the lowly nun—all I !
Ah ! now I feel it ; naught can give us peace
Mid worldly cares, nothing save only conscience !
Healthy she triumphs over wickedness,
Over dark slander ; but if in her be found
A single casual stain, then misery.
With what a deadly sore my soul doth smart ;
My heart, with venom filled, doth like a hammer
Beat in mine ears reproach ; all things revolt me,
And my head whirls, and in my eyes are children
Dripping with blood ; and gladly would I flee,
But nowhere can find refuge—horrible !
Pitiful he whose conscience is unclean !

TAVERN ON THE LITHUANIAN
FRONTIER

MISSAIL and VARLAAM, wandering friars ;
GREGORY in secular attire ; HOSTESS

HOSTESS. With what shall I regale you, my reverend honoured guests ?

VARLAAM. With what God sends, little hostess. Have you no wine ?

HOSTESS. As if I had not, my fathers ! I will bring it at once.   (*Exit.*)

MISSAIL. Why so glum, comrade ? Here is that very Lithuanian frontier which you so wished to reach.

GREGORY. Until I shall be in Lithuania, till then I shall not be content.

VARLAAM. What is it that makes you so fond of Lithuania ? Here are we, Father Missail and I, a sinner, when we fled from the monastery, then we cared for nothing. Was it

Lithuania, was it Russia, was it fiddle, was it dulcimer ?
All the same for us, if only there was wine. That's the
main thing !

MISSAIL. Well said, Father Varlaam.

HOSTESS. (*Enters.*)
There you are, my fathers. Drink to your health.

MISSAIL. Thanks, my good friend. God bless thee. (*The
monks drink. Varlaam trolls a ditty:* " *Thou passest
by, my dear,*" *etc.*) (*To* GREGORY) Why don't you join
in the song ? Not even join in the song ?

GREGORY. I don't wish to.

MISSAIL. Everyone to his liking——

VARLAAM. But a tipsy man's in Heaven. * Father Missail !
we will drink a glass to our hostess. (*Sings:* " *Where
the brave lad in durance,*" *etc.*) Still, Father Missail,
when I am drinking, then I don't like sober men ; tipsi-
ness is one thing—but pride quite another. If you want
to live as we do, you are welcome. No ?—then take
yourself off, away with you ; a mountebank is no companion for a priest.

---

* The Russian text has here a play on the words which cannot be
satisfactorily rendered into English.

GREGORY. Drink, and keep your thoughts to yourself, * Father Varlaam! You see, I too sometimes know how to make puns.

VARLAAM. But why should I keep my thoughts to myself?

MISSAIL. Let him alone, Father Varlaam.

VARLAAM. But what sort of a fasting man is he? Of his own accord he attached himself as a companion to us; no one knows who he is, no one knows whence he comes— and yet he gives himself grand airs; perhaps he has a close acquaintance with the pillory. (*Drinks and sings:* "*A young monk took the tonsure,*" etc.)

GREGORY. (*To* HOSTESS.) Whither leads this road?

HOSTESS. To Lithuania, my dear, to the Luyóv mountains.

GREGORY. And is it far to the Luyóv mountains?

HOSTESS. Not far; you might get there by evening, but for the tsar's frontier barriers, and the captains of the guard.

GREGORY. What say you? Barriers! What means this?

---

* The Russian text has here a play on the words which cannot be satisfactorily rendered into English.

HOSTESS. Someone has escaped from Moscow, and orders have been given to detain and search everyone.

GREGORY. (*Aside.*) Here's a pretty mess!

VARLAAM. Hallo, comrade! You've been making up to mine hostess. To be sure you don't want vodka, but you want a young woman. All right, brother, all right! Everyone has his own ways, and Father Missail and I have only one thing which we care for—we drink to the bottom, we drink; turn it upside down, and knock at the bottom.

MISSAIL. Well said, Father Varlaam.

GREGORY. (*To* HOSTESS.) Whom do they want? Who escaped from Moscow?

HOSTESS. God knows; a thief perhaps, a robber. But here even good folk are worried now. And what will come of it? Nothing. They will not catch the old devil; as if there were no other road into Lithuania than the highway! Just turn to the left from here, then by the pinewood or by the footpath as far as the chapel on the Chekansky brook, and then straight across the marsh to Khlopin, and thence to Zakhariev, and then any child will guide you to the Luyóv mountains. The only good of these inspectors is to worry passers-by and rob us poor folk. (*A noise is heard.*) What's that? Ah, there they are, curse them! They are going their rounds.

GREGORY. Hostess! is there another room in the cottage?

HOSTESS. No, my dear; I should be glad myself to hide. But they are only pretending to go their rounds; but give them wine and bread, and Heaven knows what— May perdition take them, the accursed ones! May——
(*Enter* OFFICERS.)

OFFICERS. Good health to you, mine hostess!

HOSTESS. You are kindly welcome, dear guests.

AN OFFICER. (*To another.*) Ha, there's drinking going on here; we shall get something here. (*To the* Monks.) Who are you?

VARLAAM. We—are two old clerics, humble monks; we are going from village to village, and collecting Christian alms for the monastery.

OFFICER. (*To* GREGORY.) And thou?

MISSAIL. Our comrade.

GREGORY. A layman from the suburb ; I have conducted the old men as far as the frontier ; from here I am going to my own home.

MISSAIL. So you have changed your mind ?

GREGORY. (*Sotto voce.*) Be silent.

OFFICER. Hostess, bring some more wine, and we will drink here a little and talk a little with these old men.

2ND OFFICER. (*Sotto voce.*) Yon lad, it appears, is poor ; there' nothing to be got out of him ; on the other hand the old men——

1ST OFFICER. Be silent ; we shall come to them presently. —Well, my fathers, how are you getting on ?

VARLAAM. Badly, my sons, badly ! The Christians have now turned stingy ; they love their money ; they hide their money. They give little to God. The people of the world have become great sinners. They have all devoted themselves to commerce, to earthly cares ; they think of worldly wealth, not of the salvation of the soul. You walk and walk ; you beg and beg ; sometimes in three days begging will not bring you three half-pence. What a sin ! A week goes by ; another week ; you look into your bag, and there is so little in it that you are ashamed to show yourself at the monastery. What are you to do ? From very sorrow you drink away what is left ; a real calamity ! Ah, it is bad ! It seems our last days have come——

HOSTESS. (*Weeps.*) God pardon and save you !
> (*During the course of* VARLAAM'S *speech the* 1st
> OFFICER *watches* MISSAIL *significantly.*)

1ST OFFICER. Alexis ! have you the tsar's edict with you ?

2ND OFFICER. I have it.

1ST OFFICER. Give it here.

MISSAIL. Why do you look at me so fixedly ?

1ST OFFICER. This is why ; from Moscow there has fled a certain wicked heretic—Grishka Otrepiev. Have you heard this ?

MISSAIL. I have not heard it.

OFFICER. Not heard it ? Very good. And the tsar has ordered to arrest and hang the fugitive heretic. Do you know this ?

MISSAIL. I do not know it.

OFFICER. (*To* VARLAAM.) Do you know how to read ?

VARLAAM. In my youth I knew how, but I have forgotten.

OFFICER. (*To* MISSAIL.) And thou ?

MISSAIL. God has not made me wise.

OFFICER. So then here's the tsar's edict.

MISSAIL. What do I want it for ?

OFFICER. It seems to me that this fugitive heretic, thief, swindler, is—thou.

MISSAIL. I ? Good gracious ! What are you talking about ?

OFFICER. Stay ! Hold the doors. Then we shall soon get at the truth.

HOSTESS. O the cursèd tormentors ! Not to leave even the old man in peace !

OFFICER. Which of you here is a scholar ?

GREGORY. (*Comes forward.*) I am a scholar !

OFFICER. Oh, indeed ! And from whom did you learn ?

GREGORY. From our sacristan.

OFFICER (*Gives him the edict.*) Read it aloud.

GREGORY. (*Reads.*) " An unworthy monk of the Monastery of Chudov, Gregory, of the family of Otrepiev, has fallen into heresy, taught by the devil, and has dared to vex the holy brotherhood by all kinds of iniquities and acts of lawlessness. And, according to information, it has been shown that he, the accursed Grishka, has fled to the Lithuanian frontier."

OFFICER. (*To* MISSAIL.) How can it be anyone but you ?

GREGORY. " And the tsar has commanded to arrest him——"

OFFICER. And to hang !

GREGORY. It does not say here " to hang."

OFFICER. Thou liest. What is meant is not always put into writing. Read : to arrest and to hang.

GREGORY. " And to hang. And the age of the thief Grishka " (*looking at* VARLAAM) " about fifty, and his height medium ; he has a bald head, grey beard, fat belly."

(*All glance at* VARLAAM.)

1st Officer. My lads! Here is Grishka! Hold him! bind him! I never thought to catch him so quickly.

Varlaam. (*Snatching the paper.*) Hands off, my lads! What sort of a Grishka am I? What! fifty years old, grey beard, fat belly! No, brother. You're too young to play off tricks on me. I have not read for a long time and I make it out badly, but I shall manage to make it out, as it's a hanging matter. (*Spells it out.*) " And his age twenty." Why, brother, where does it say fifty ?— Do you see—twenty?

2nd Officer. Yes, I remember, twenty; even so it was told us.

1st Officer. (*To* Gregory.) Then, evidently, you like a joke, brother.

> (*During the reading* Gregory *stands with downcast head, and his hand in his breast.*)

Varlaam. (*Continues.*) " And in stature he is small, chest broad, one arm shorter than the other, blue eyes, red hair, a wart on his cheek, another on his forehead." Then is it not you, my friend?

> (Gregory *suddenly draws a dagger; all give way before him; he dashes through the window.*)

Officers. Hold him! Hold him!

> (*All run out in disorder.*)

MOSCOW. SHUISKY'S HOUSE

SHUISKY. A number of Guests. Supper

SHUISKY. More wine ! Now, my dear guests.

(*He rises ; all rise after him.*)

The final draught !

Read the prayer, boy.

BOY.   Lord of the heavens, Who art
Eternally and everywhere, accept
The prayer of us Thy servants.   For our monarch,
By Thee appointed, for our pious tsar,
Of all good Christians autocrat, we pray.
Preserve him in the palace, on the field
Of battle, on his nightly couch ; grant to him
Victory o'er his foes ; from sea to sea
May he be glorified ; may all his house
Blossom with health, and may its precious branches
O'ershadow all the earth ; to us, his slaves,
May he, as heretofore, be generous.
Gracious, long-suffering, and may the founts
Of his unfailing wisdom flow upon us ;
Raising the royal cup, Lord of the heavens,
For this we pray.

D

SHUISKY. (*Drinks.*) Long live our mighty sovereign!
     Farewell, dear guests.   I thank you that ye scorned not
My bread and salt.   Farewell; good-night.
                         (*Exeunt* Guests : *he conducts them to the door.*)

PÚSHKIN.   Hardly could they tear themselves away; indeed,
     Prince Vassíly Ivanovitch, I began to think that we
     should not succeed in getting any private talk.

SHUISKY. (*To the* Servants.) You there, why do you stand
     gaping? Always eavesdropping on gentlemen! Clear
     the table, and then be off.

                                   (*Exeunt* Servants.)
                         What   is it, Athanasius

     Mikaílovitch?

PÚSHKIN.   Such a wondrous thing!
     A message was sent here to me to-day
     From Crácow by my nephew Gabriel Púshkin.

SHUISKY.   Well?

PÚSHKIN.   'Tis strange news my nephew writes.   The son
     Of the Terrible—   But stay——
                         (*Goes to the door and examines it.*)
                                   The royal boy,
     Who murdered was by order of Borís——

SHUISKY.   But these are no new tidings.

PÚSHKIN.   Wait a little;
    Dimítry lives.

SHUISKY.   So that's it!   News indeed!
    Dimítry living!—really marvellous!
    And is that all?

PÚSHKIN.   Pray listen to the end;
    Whoe'er he be, whether he be Dimítry
    Rescued, or else some spirit in his shape,
    Some daring rogue, some insolent pretender,
    In any case Dimítry has appeared.

SHUISKY.   It cannot be.

PÚSHKIN.   Púshkin himself beheld him
    When first he reached the court, and through the ranks
    Of Lithuanian gentlemen went straight
    Into the secret chamber of the king.

SHUISKY.   What kind of man?   Whence comes he?

PÚSHKIN.   No one knows.
    'Tis known that he was Vishnevétsky's servant;
    That to a ghostly father on a bed
    Of sickness he disclosed himself; possessed
    Of this strange secret, his proud master nursed him,
    From his sick bed upraised him, and straightway
    Took him to Sigismund.

SHUISKY.   And what say men
  Of this bold fellow ?

PÚSHKIN.   'Tis said that he is wise,
  Affable, cunning, popular with all men.
  He has bewitched the fugitives from Moscow,
  The Catholic priests see eye to eye with him.
  The King caresses him, and, it is said,
  Has promised help.

SHUISKY.   All this is such a medley
  That my head whirls.   Brother, beyond all doubt
  This man is a pretender, but the danger
  Is, I confess, not slight.   This is grave news !
  And if it reach the people, then there'll be
  A mighty tempest.

PÚSHKIN.   Such a storm that hardly
  Will Tsar Borís contrive to keep the crown
  Upon his clever head ; and losing it
  Will get but his deserts !   He governs us
  As did the tsar Iván of evil memory.
  What profits it that public executions
  Have ceased, that we no longer sing in public
  Hymns to Christ Jesus on the field of blood ;
  That we no more are burnt in public places,
  Or that the tsar no longer with his sceptre

Rakes in the ashes ? Is there any safety
In our poor life ? Each day disgrace awaits us ;
The dungeon or Siberia, cowl or fetters,
And then in some deaf nook a starving death,
Or else the halter. Where are the most renowned
Of all our houses, where the Sitsky princes,
Where are the Shestunóvs, where the Románovs,
Hope of our fatherland ? Imprisoned, tortured,
In exile. Do but wait, and a like fate
Will soon be thine. Think of it ! Here at home,
Just as in Lithuania, we're beset
By treacherous slaves—and tongues are ever ready
For base betrayal, thieves bribed by the State.
We hang upon the word of the first servant
Whom we may please to punish. Then he bethought him
To take from us our privilege of hiring
Our serfs at will ; we are no longer masters
Of our own lands. Presume not to dismiss
An idler. Willy nilly, thou must feed him !
Presume not to outbid a man in hiring
A labourer, or you will find yourself
In the Court's clutches.—Was such an evil heard of
Even under tsar Iván ? And are the people
The better off ? Ask them. Let the pretender
But promise them the old free right of transfer,
Then there'll be sport.

SHUISKY. Thou'rt right ; but be advised ;
Of this, of all things, for a time we'll speak
No word.

PÚSHKIN. Assuredly, keep thine own counsel.
Thou art—a person of discretion ; always
I am glad to commune with thee ; and if aught
At any time disturbs me, I endure not
To keep it from thee ; and, truth to tell, thy mead
And velvet ale to-day have so untied
My tongue . . . Farewell then, prince.

SHUISKY. Brother, farewell.
Farewell, my brother, till we meet again.

(He escorts PÚSHKIN *out.)*

PALACE OF THE TSAR

The TSARÉVICH is drawing a map. The
TSARÉVNA. The NURSE of the Tsarévna

KSENIA. (*Kisses a portrait.*) My dear bridegroom, come'y
son of a king, not to me wast thou given, not to thy
affianced bride, but to a dark sepulchre in a strange
land; never shall I take comfort, ever shall I weep for
thee.

NURSE. Eh, tsarévna! a maiden weeps as the dew fal's;
the sun will rise, will dry the dew. Thou wilt have
another bridegroom—and handsome and affable. My
charming child, thou wilt learn to ove him, thou wilt
forget Iván the king's son.

KSENIA. Nay, nurse, I will be true to him even in death.

(BORÍS *enters.*)

TSAR. What, Ksenia? What, my sweet one? In thy
girlhood
Already a woe-stricken widow, ever
Bewailing thy dead bridegroom! Fate forbade me

To be the author of thy bliss.   Perchance
I angered Heaven; it was no mine to compass
Thy happiness.   Innocent one, for what
Art thou a sufferer ?   And thou, my son,
With what art thou employed ?   What's this ?

FEÓDOR.   A chart
Of all the land of Muscovy ; our tsardom
From end to end.   Here you see ; there is Moscow,
There Nóvgorod, there Astrakhan.   Here lies
The sea, here the dense forest tract of Perm,
And here Siberia.

TSAR.   And what is this
Which makes a winding pattern here ?

FEÓDOR.   That is
The Volga.

TSAR.   Very good !   Here's the sweet fruit
Of learning.   One can view as from the clouds
Our whole dominion at a glance ; its frontiers,
Its towns, its rivers.   Learn, my son ; 'tis science
Which gives to us an abstract of the events
Of our swift-flowing life.   Some day, perchance
Soon, all the lands which thou so cunningly

To-day hast drawn on paper, all will come
Under thy hand. Learn, therefore ; and more smoothly,
More clearly wilt thou take, my son, upon thee
The cares of state.

              (SEMYÓN GODUNÓV *enters.*)
              But there comes Godunóv

Bringing 'eports to me. (*To* KSENIA.) Go to thy
  chamber
Dearest ; farewell, my child ; God comfort thee.

              (*Exeunt* KSENIA *and* NURSE.)

What news hast thou for me, Semyón Nikítich ?

SEMYÓN G. To-day at dawn the butler of Prince Shuisky
And Púshkin's servant brought me information.

TSAR. Well ?

SEMYÓN G. In the first place Púshkin's man deposed
That yestermorn came to his house from Crácow
A courier, who within an hour was sent
Without a letter back.

TSAR.   Arrest the courier.

SEMYÓN G. Some are already sent to overtake him.

TSAR. And what of Shuisky ?

SEMYÓN G. Last night he entertained
His friends; the Búturlins, both Miloslávskys,
And Saltikóv, with Púshkin and some others.
They parted late. Púshkin alone remained
Closeted with his host and talked with him
A long time more.

TSAR. For Shuisky send forthwith.

SEMYÓN G. Sire, he is here already.

TSAR. Call him hither.

(*Exit* SEMYÓN GODUNÓV.)

Dealings with Lithuania ? What means this ?
I like not the seditious race of Púshkins,
Nor must I trust in Shuisky, obsequious,
But bold and wily—

(*Enter* SHUISKY.)
Prince, I must speak with thee.
But thou thyself, it seems, hast business with me,
And I would listen first to thee.

SHUISKY. Yea, sire ;
It is my duty to convey to thee
Grave news.

TSAR. I listen.

SHUISKY. (*Sotto voce, pointing to* FEÓDOR.)
                    But, sire——

TSAR.   The tsarévich
    May learn whate'er Prince Shuisky knoweth.   Speak.

SHUISKY.   My liege, from Lithuania there have come
    Tidings to us——

TSAR.   Are they not those same tidings
    Which yestereve a courier bore to Púshkin ?

SHUISKY.   Nothing is hidden from him !—Sire, I thought
    Thou knew'st not yet this secret.

TSAR.   Let not that
    Trouble thee, prince ; I fain would scrutinise
    Thy information ; else we shall not learn
    The actual truth.

SHUISKY.   I know this only, Sire ;
    In Crácow a pretender hath appeared ;
    The king and nobles back him.

TSAR.   What say they ?
    And who is this pretender ?

SHUISKY.   I know not.

TSAR.   But wherein is he dangerous ?

SHUISKY.   Verily

    Thy state, my liege, is firm ; by graciousness,
    Zeal, bounty, thou hast won the filial love
    Of all thy slaves ; but thou thyself dost know
    The mob is thoughtless, changeable, rebellious,
    Credulous, lightly given to vain hope,
    Obedient to each momentary impulse,
    To truth deaf and indifferent ; it feedeth
    On fables ; shameless boldness pleaseth it.
    So, if this unknown vagabond should cross
    The Lithuanian border, Dimítry's name
    Raised from the grave will gain him a whole crowd
    Of fools.

TSAR.   Dimítry's ?—What ?—That child's ?—Dimí ry's ?
    Withdraw, tsarévich.

SHUISKY.   He flushed ; there'll be a storm !

FEÓDOR.   Suffer me, Sire——

TSAR.   Impossible, my son ;
    Go, go !

                                  (*Exit* FEÓDOR.)
    Dimítry's name !

SHUISKY.   Then he knew nothing.

TSAR.   Listen : take steps this very hour that Russia
        Be fenced by barriers from Lithuania ;
        That not a single soul pass o'er the border,
        That not a hare run o'er to us from Poland,
        Nor crow fly here from Crácow.   Away !

SHUISKY.   I go.

TSAR.   Stay !—Is it not a fact that this report
        Is artfully concocted ?   Hast ever heard
        That dead men have arisen from their graves
        To question tsars, legitimate tsars, appointed,
        Chosen by the voice of all the people, crowned
        By the great Patriarch ?   Is't not laughable ?
        Eh ?   What ?   Why laugh'st thou not thereat ?

SHUISKY.   I, Sire ?

TSAR.   Hark, Prince Vassíly ; when first I learned this child
        Had been—this child had somehow lost its life,
        'Twas thou I sent to search the matter out.
        Now by the Cross and God I do adjure thee,
        Declare to me the truth upon thy conscience ;
        Didst recognise the slaughtered boy ; was't not
        A substitute ?   Reply.

SHUISKY.   I swear to thee——

TSAR.   Nay, Shuisky, swear not, but reply; was it
    Indeed Dimítry ?

SHUISKY.   He.

TSAR.   Consider, prince.
    I promise clemency; I will not punish
    With vain disgrace a lie that's past. But if
    Thou now beguile me, then by my son's head
    I swear—an evil fate shall overtake thee,
    Requital such that Tsar Iván Vasílievich
    Shall shudder in his grave with horror of it.

SHUISKY. In punishment no terror lies; the terror
    Doth lie in thy disfavour; in thy presence
    Dare I use cunning? Could I deceive myself
    So blindly as not recognise Dimítry ?
    Three days in the cathedral did I visit
    His corpse, escorted thither by all Úglich.
    Around him thirteen bodies lay of those
    Slain by the people, and on them corruption
    Already had set in perceptibly.
    But lo! the childish face of the tsarévich
    Was bright and fresh and quiet as if asleep;
    The deep gash had congealed not, nor the lines
    Of his face even altered.   No, my liege,
    There is no doubt; Dimítry sleeps in the grave.

TSAR. Enough, withdraw.

(*Exit* SHUISKY.)

I choke !—let me get my breath !
I felt it ; all my blood surged to my face,
And heavily fell back.—So that is why
For thirteen years together I have dreamed
Ever about the murdered child.   Yes, yes—
'Tis that !—now I perceive.   But who is he,
My terrible antagonist ?   Who is it
Opposeth me ?   An empty name, a shadow.
Can it be a shade shall tear from me the purple,
A sound deprive my children of succession ?
Fool that I was !   Of what was I afraid ?
Blow on this phantom—and it is no more.
So, I am fast resolved ; I'll show no sign
Of fear, but nothing must be held in scorn.
Ah ! heavy art thou, crown of Monomákh !

CRÁCOW.   HOUSE OF VISHNEVÉTSKY

The PRETENDER and a CATHOLIC PRIEST

PRETENDER.   Nay, father, there will be no trouble.   I know
The spirit of my people ; piety
Does not run wild in them, their tsar's example
To them is sacred.   Furthermore, the people
Are always tolerant.   I warrant you,
Before two years my people all, and all
The Eastern Church, will recognise the power
Of Peter's Vicar.

PRIEST.   May Saint Ignatius aid thee
When other times shall come.   Meanwhile, tsarévich,
Hide in thy soul the seed of heavenly blessing ;
Religious duty bids us oft dissemble
Before the blabbing world ; the people judge
Thy words, thy deeds ; God only sees thy motives.

PRETENDER.   Amen.   Who's there ?

(Enter a Servant.)
Say that we will receive them.
*(The doors are opened ; a crowd of Russians and Poles
enters.)*

Comrades !   To morrow we depart from Crácow.
Mníshek, with thee for three days in Sambór
I'll stay.   I know thy hospitable castle
Both shines in splendid stateliness, and glories
In its young mistress.   There I hope to see
Charming Marina.   And ye, my friends, ye, Russia
And Lithuania, ye who have upraised
Fraternal banners against a common foe,
Against mine enemy, yon crafty villain,
Ye sons of Slavs, speedily will I lead
Your dread battalions to the longed-for conflict.
But soft !   Methinks among you I descry
New faces.

GABRIEL P.   They have come to beg for sword
And service with your Grace.

PRETENDER.   Welcome, my lads.
You are friends to me.   But tell me, Púshkin, who
Is this fine fellow ?

PÚSHKIN.   Prince Kúrbsky.

PRETENDER.   (*To* KÚRBSKY.)   A famous name !
Art kinsman to the hero of Kazán ?

KÚRBSKY.   His son.

E

PRETENDER.   **Liveth** he still ?

KÚRBSKY.   Nay, he is dead.

PRETENDER.   A noble soul !   A man of war and counsel.
      But from the time when he appeared beneath
      The ancient town Olgín with the Lithuanians,
      Hardy avenger of his injuries,
      Rumour hath held her tongue concerning him.

KÚRBSKY.   My father led the remnant of his life
      On lands bestowed upon him by Batóry ;
      There, in Volhynia, solitary and quiet,
      Sought consolation for himself in studies ;
      But peaceful labour did not comfort him ;
      He ne'er forgot the home of his young days,
      And to the end pined for it.

PRETENDER.   Hapless chieftain !
      How brightly shone the dawn of his resounding
      And stormy life !   Glad am I, noble knight,
      That now his blood is reconciled in thee
      To his fatherland.   The faults of fathers must not
      Be called to mind.   Peace to their grave.   Approach ;
      Give me thy hand !   Is it not strange ?—the son
      Of Kúrbsky to the throne is leading—whom ?
      Whom but Iván's own son ?—All favours me ;
      People and fate alike.—Say, who art thou ?

A POLE. Sobánsky, a free noble.

PRETENDER.   Praise and honour
 Attend thee, child of liberty. Give him
 A third of his full pay beforehand.—Who
 Are these ? On them I recognise the dress
 Of my own country. These are ours.

KRUSHCHOV. (*Bows low.*)   Yea, Sire,
 Our father ; we are thralls of thine, devoted
 And persecuted ; we have fled from Moscow,
 Disgraced, to thee our tsar, and for thy sake
 Are ready to lay down our lives ; our corpses
 Shall be for thee steps to the royal throne.

PRETENDER. Take heart, innocent sufferers. Only let me
 Reach Moscow, and, once there, Borís shall settle
 Some scores with me and you. What news of Moscow ?

KRUSHCHOV. As yet all there is quiet. But already
 The folk have got to know that the tsarévich
 Was saved ; already everywhere is read
 Thy proclamation. All are waiting for thee.
 Not long ago Borís sent two boyárs
 To execution merely because in secret
 They drank thy health.

PRETENDER.   O hapless, good boyárs!
   But blood for blood! and woe to Godunóv!
   What do they say of him?

KRUSHCHOV.   He has withdrawn
   Into his gloomy palace.   He is grim
   And sombre.   Executions loom ahead.
   But sickness gnaws him.   Hardly hath he strength
   To drag himself along, and—it is thought—
   His last hour is already not far off.

PRETENDER.   A speedy death I wish him, as becomes
   A great-souled foe to wish.   If not, then woe
   To the miscreant!—And whom doth he intend
   To name as his successor?

KRUSHCHOV.   He shows not
   His purposes, but it would seem he destines
   Feódor, his young son, to be our tsar.

PRETENDER.   His reckonings, maybe, will yet prove wrong.
   Who art thou?

KARÉLA.   A Cossack; from the Don I am sent
   To thee, from the free troops, from the brave hetmen
   From upper and lower regions of the Cossacks,
   To look upon thy bright and royal eyes,
   And tender thee their homage.

PRETENDER. Well I knew
The men of Don; I doubted not to see
The Cossack hetmen in my ranks. We thank
Our army of the Don. To-day, we know,
The Cossacks are unjustly persecuted,
Oppressed; but if God grant us to ascend
The throne of our forefathers, then as of yore
We'll gratify the free and faithful Don.

POET. (*Approaches, bowing low, and taking Gregory by the
hem of his caftan.*)
Great prince, illustrious offspring of a king!

PRETENDER. What wouldst thou?

POET. Condescendingly accept
This poor fruit of my earnest toil.

PRETENDER. What see I?
Verses in Latin! Blest a hundredfold
The tie of sword and lyre; the selfsame laurel
Binds them in friendship. I was born beneath
A northern sky, but yet the Latin muse
To me is a familiar voice; I love
The blossoms of Parnassus, I believe
The prophecies of singers. Not in vain

The ecstasy boils in their flaming breast;
Action is hallowed, being glorified
Beforehand by the poets!   Approach, my friend.
In memory of me accept this gift.

(Gives him a ring.)

When fate fulfils for me her covenant,
When I assume the crown of my forefathers,
I hope again to hear the measured tones
Of thy sweet voice, and thy inspirèd lay.
Musa gloriam coronat, gloriaque musam.
And so, friends, till to-morrow, *au revoir.*

ALL.   Forward!   Long live Dimítry!   Forward, forward!
Long live Dimítry, the great prince of Moscow!

CASTLE OF THE GOVERNOR
MNÍSHEK IN SAMBÓR

Dressing-Room of Marina

MARINA, ROUZYA (dressing her), **Serving-Women**

MARINA. (*Before a mirror.*) Now then, is it ready ? Cannot
you make haste ?

ROUZYA. I pray you first to make the difficult choice ;
Will you the necklace wear of pearls, or else
The emerald half-moon ?

MARINA.   My diamond crown.

ROUZYA. Splendid ! Do you remember that you wore it
When to the palace you were pleased to go ?
They say that at the ball your gracious h ghness
Shone like the sun ; men sighed, fair ladies whispered—
'Twas then that for the first time young Khotkévich
Beheld you, he who after shot himself.
And whosoever looked on you, they say
That instant fell in love.

MARINA.   Can't you be quicker ?

ROUZYA.   At once.   To-day your father counts upon you.
    'Twas not for naught the young tsarévich saw you ;
    He could not hide his rapture ; wounded he is
    Already ; so it only needs to deal him
    A resolute blow, and instantly, my lady,
    He'll be in love with you.   'Tis now a month
    Since, quitting Crácow, heedless of the war
    And throne of Moscow, he has feasted here,
    Your guest, enraging Poles alike and Russians.
    Heavens !   Shall I ever live to see the day ?—
    Say, you will not, when to his capital
    Dimítry leads the queen of Moscow, say
    You'll not forsake me ?

MARINA.   Dost thou truly think
    I shall be queen ?

ROUZYA.   Who, if not you ?   Who here
    Dares to compare in beauty with my mistress ?
    The race of Mníshek never yet has yielded
    To any.   In intellect you are beyond
    All praise.—Happy the suitor whom your glance
    Honours with its regard, who wins your heart—
    Whoe'er he be, be he our king, the dauphin
    Of France, or even this our poor tsarévich
    God knows who, God knows whence !

MARINA.   The very son
Of the tsar, and so confessed by the whole world.

ROUZYA.   And yet last winter he was but a servant
In the house of Vishnevétsky.

MARINA.   He was hiding.

ROUZYA.   I do not question it : but still do you know
What people say about him ?   That perhaps
He is a deacon run away from Moscow,
In his own district a notorious rogue.

MARINA.   What nonsense !

ROUZYA.   O, I do not credit it !
I only say he ought to bless his fate
That you have so preferred him to the others.

WAITING-WOMAN.   (*Runs in.*)   The guests have come already.

MARINA.   There you see ;
You're ready to chatter silliness till daybreak.
Meanwhile I am not dressed——

ROUZYA.   Within a moment
'Twill be quite ready.

                    (*The* Waiting-women *bustle.*)

MARINA.   (*Aside.*)   I must find out all.

A SUITE OF LIGHTED ROOMS. Music

VISHNEVÉTSKY, MNÍSHEK

MNÍSHEK.   With none but my Marina doth he speak,
With no one else consorteth—and that business
Looks dreadfully like marriage.   Now confess,
Didst ever think my daughter would be a queen ?

VISHNEVÉTSKY.   'Tis wonderful.—And, Mníshek, didst thou
think
My servant would ascend the throne of Moscow ?

MNÍSHEK.   And what a girl, look you, is my Marina.
I merely hinted to her : " Now, be careful !
Let not Dimítry slip "—and lo ! already
He is completely tangled in her toils.
       (*The band plays a Polonaise.   The* PRETENDER *and*
       MARINA *advance as the first couple.*)

MARINA.   (*Sotto voce to* DIMÍTRY.)   To-morrow evening at
eleven, beside
The fountain in the avenue of lime-trees.
                              (*They walk off.   A second couple.*)

CAVALIER. What can Dimítry see in her ?

DAME. How say you ?
She is a beauty.

CAVALIER. Yes, a marble nymph ;
Eyes, lips, devoid of life, without a smile.

(*A fresh couple.*)

DAME. He is not handsome, but his eyes are pleasing,
And one can see he is of royal birth.

(*A fresh couple.*)

DAME. When will the army march ?

CAVALIER. When the tsarévich
Orders it ; we are ready ; but 'tis clear
The lady Mníshek and Dimítry mean
To keep us prisoners here.

DAME. A pleasant durance.

CAVALIER. Truly, if you . . .

(*They walk off ; the rooms become empty.*)

MNÍSHEK. We old ones dance no longer ;
The sound of music lures us not ; we press not
Nor kiss the hands of charmers—ah ! my friend,
I've not forgotten the old pranks ! Things now

Are not what once they were, what once they were !
Youth, I'll be sworn, is not so bold, nor beauty
So lively ; everything—confess, my friend—
Has somehow become dull.   So let us leave them ;
My comrade, let us go and find a flask
Of old Hungarian overgrown with mould ;
Let's bid my butler open an old bottle,
And in a quiet corner, *tête-à-tête*,
Let's drain a draught, a stream as thick as fat ;
And while we're so engaged, let's think things over.
Let us go, brother.

VISHNEVÉTSKY.   Yes, my friend, let's go.

NIGHT

THE GARDEN. THE FOUNTAIN

PRETENDER. (*Enters.*) Here is the fountain; hither will
    she come.
  I was not born a coward ; I have seen
  Death near at hand, and face to face with death
  My spirit hath not blenched.   A life-long dungeon
  Hath threatened me, I have been close pursued,
  And yet my spirit quailed not, and by boldness
  I have escaped captivity.   But what
  Is this which now constricts my breath ? What means
  This overpowering tremor, or this quivering
  Of tense desire ?   No, this is fear.   All day
  I have waited for this secret meeting, pondered
  On all that I should say to her, how best
  I might enmesh Marina's haughty mind,
  Calling her queen of Moscow.   But the hour
  Has come—and I remember naught, I cannot
  Recall the speeches I have learned by rote ;
  Love puts imagination to confusion—
  But something there gleamed suddenly—a rustling ;
  Hush—no, it was the moon's deceitful light,
  It was the rustling of the breeze.

MARINA. (*Enters.*)   Tsarévich !

PRETENDER. 'Tis she. Now all the blood in me stands still.

MARINA. Dimítry ! Is it thou ?

PRETENDER.   Bewitching voice !

                               (*Goes to her.*)

   Is it thou, at last ?   Is it thou I see, alone
   With me, beneath the roof of quiet night ?
   How s'owly passed the tedious day ! How slowly
   The glow of evening died away ! How long
   I have waited in the gloom of night !

MARINA.   The hours
   Are flitting fast, and time is precious to me.
   I did not grant a meeting here to thee
   To listen to a lover's tender speeches.
   No need of words. I well believe thou lovest ;
   But listen ; with thy stormy, doubtful fate
   I have resolved to join my own ; but one thing,
   Dimítry, I require ; I claim that thou
   Disclose to me thy secret hopes, thy plans,
   Even thy fears, that hand in hand with thee
   I may confront life boldly—not in blindness
   Of childlike ignorance, not as the slave

And plaything of my husband's light desires,
Thy speechless concubine, but as thy spouse,
And worthy helpmate of the tsar of Moscow.

PRETENDER. O, if it be only for one short hour,
Forget the cares and troubles of my fate !
Forget 'tis the tsarévich whom thou seest
Before thee. O, behold in me, Marina,
A lover, by thee chosen, happy only
In thy regard. O, listen to the prayers
Of love ! Grant me to utter all wherewith
My heart is full.

MARINA.   Prince, this is not the time ;
Thou loiterest, and meanwhile the devotion
Of thine adherents cooleth. Hour by hour
Danger becomes more dangerous, difficulties
More difficult ; already dubious rumours
Are current, novelty already takes
The place of novelty ; and Godunóv
Adopts his measures.

PRETENDER.   What is Godunóv ?
Is thy sweet love, my only blessedness,
Swayed by Borís ? Nay, nay. Indifferently
I now regard his throne, his kingly power.

Thy love—without it what to me is life,
And glory's glitter, and the state of Russia ?
On the dull steppe, in a poor mud hut, thou—
Thou wilt requite me for the kingly crown ;
Thy love——

MARINA.   For shame !   Forget not, prince, thy high
    And sacred destiny ; thy dignity
    Should be to thee more dear than all the joys
    Of life and its allurements.   It thou canst not
    With anything compare.   Not to a boy,
    Insanely boiling, captured by my beauty—
    But to the heir of Moscow's throne give I
    My hand in solemn wise, to the tsarévich
    Rescued by destiny.

PRETENDER.   Torture me not,
    Charming Marina ; say not that 'twas my rank
    And not myself that thou didst choose.   Marina !
    Thou knowest not how sorely thou dost wound
    My heart thereby.   What if—O fearful doubt !—
    Say, if blind destiny had not assigned me
    A kingly birth ; if I were not indeed
    Son of Iván, were not this boy, so long
    Forgotten by the world—say, then wouldst thou
    Have loved me ?

MARINA.   Thou art Dimítry, and aught else
 Thou canst not be ; it is not possible
 For me to love another.

PRETENDER.   Nay ! enough —
 I have no wish to share with a dead body
 A mistress who belongs to him ; I have done
 With counterfeiting, and will tell the truth.
 Know, then, that thy Dimítry long ago
 Perished, was buried—and will not rise again ;
 And dost thou wish to know what man I am ?
 Well, I will tell thee. I am—a poor monk.
 Grown weary of monastic servitude,
 I pondered 'neath the cowl my bold design,
 Made ready for the world a miracle—
 And from my cell at last fled to the Cossacks,
 To their wild hovels ; there I learned to handle
 Both steeds and swords ; I showed myself to you.
 I called myself Dimítry, and deceived
 The brainless Poles. What say'st thou, proud **Marina** ?
 Art thou content with my confession ? Why
 Dost thou keep silence ?

MARINA.   O shame ! O woe is me !
              (Silence.,
        F

PRETENDER. (*Sotto voce.*) O whither hath a fit of anger
    led me ?
    The happiness devised with so much labour
    I have, perchance, destroyed for ever.   Idiot,
    What have I done ?   (*Aloud.*)   I see thou art ashamed
    Of love not princely ; so pronounce on me
    The fatal word ; my fate is in thy hands.
    Decide ; I wait.

                                        (*Falls on his knees.*)

MARINA.   Rise, poor pretender !   Think'st thou
    To p'ease with genuflex ons my vain heart,
    As if I were a weak, confiding girl ?
    You err, my friend ; prone at my feet I've seen
    Kn'ghts and counts nobly born ; but not for th's
    Did I reject their prayers, that a poor monk——

PRETENDER. (*Rises.*)   Scorn not the young pretender ; noble
    virtues
    May lie perchance in him, virtues well worthy
    Of Moscow's throne, even of thy priceless hand——

MARINA.   Say of a shameful noose, insolent wretch !

PRETENDER.   I am to blame ; carried away by pride
    I have deceived God and the kings—have lied
    To the world ; but it is not for thee, Marina,

To judge me ; I am guiltless before thee.
No, I could not deceive thee. Thou to me
Wast the one sacred being, before thee
I dared not to dissemble ; love alone,
Love, jealous, blind, constrained me to tell all.

MARINA. What's that to boast of, idiot ? Who demanded
Confession of thee ? If thou, a nameless vagrant
Couldst wonderfully blind two nations, then
At least thou shouldst have merited success,
And thy bold fraud secured, by constant, deep,
And lasting secrecy. Say, can I yield
Myself to thee, can I, forgetting rank
And ma den modesty, unite my fate
With thine, when thou thyself impetuously
Dost thus with such simplicity reveal
Thy shame ? It was from Love he blabbed to me !
I marvel wherefore thou hast not from friendship
Disclosed thyself ere now before my father,
Or else before our king from joy, or else
Before Prince Vishnevétsky from the zeal
Of a devoted servant.

PRETENDER.   I swear to thee
That thou alone wast able to extort
My heart's confession ; I swear to thee that never,

Nowhere, not in the feast, not in the cup
Of folly, not in friendly confidence,
Not 'neath the knife nor tortures of the rack,
Shall my tongue give away these weighty secrets.

MARINA. Thou swearest! Then I must believe. Believe,
Of course! But may I learn by what thou swearest?
Is it not by the name of God, as suits
The Jesuits' devout adopted son?
Or by thy honour as a high-born knight?
Or, maybe, by thy royal word alone
As a king's son? Is it not so? Declare.

PRETENDER. (*Proudly.*) The phantom of the Terrible hath
made me
His son; from out the sepulchre hath named me
Dimítry, hath stirred up the people round me,
And hath consigned Borís to be my victim.
I am tsarévich. Enough! 'Twere shame for me
To stoop before a haughty Polish dame.
Farewell for ever; the game of bloody war,
The wide cares of my destiny, will smother,
I hope, the pangs of love. O, when the heat
Of shameful passion is o'erspent, how then
Shall I detest thee! Now I leave thee—ruin,

Or else a crown, awaits my head in Russia ;
Whether I meet with death as fits a soldier
In honourable fight, or as a miscreant
Upon the public scaffold, thou shalt not
Be my companion, nor shalt share with me
My fate ; but it may be thou shalt regret
The destiny thou hast refused.

MARINA.   But what
If I expose beforehand thy bold fraud
To all men ?

PRETENDER.   Dost thou think I fear thee ?   Think'st thou
They will believe a Polish maiden more
Than Russia's own tsarévich ?   Know, proud lady,
That neither king, nor pope, nor nobles trouble
Whether my words be true, whether I be
Dimítry or another.   What care they ?
But I provide a pretext for revolt
And war ; and this is all they need ; and thee,
Rebellious one, believe me, they will force
To hold thy peace.   Farewell.

MARINA.   Tsarévich, stay !
At last I hear the speech not of a boy,
But of a man.   It reconciles me to thee.
Prince, I forget thy senseless outburst, see

Again Dimítry. Listen; now is the time!
Hasten; delay no more, lead on thy troops
Quickly to Moscow, purge the Kremlin, take
Thy seat upon the throne of Moscow; then
Send me the nuptial envoy; but, God hears me.
Until thy foot be planted on its steps,
Until by thee Borís be overthrown,
I am not one to listen to love-speeches.

(Exit.

PRETENDER. No—easier far to strive with Godunóv,
Or play false with the Jesuits of the Court,
Than with a woman. Deuce take them; they're beyond
My power. She twists, and coils, and crawls, slips out
Of hand, she hisses, threatens, bites. Ah, serpent!
Serpent! 'Twas not for nothing that I trembled.
She well-nigh ruined me; but I'm resolved;
At daybreak I will put my troops in motion.

THE LITHUANIAN FRONTIER

(OCTOBER 16TH, 1604)

PRINCE KÚRBSKY and PRETENDER, both on horseback. Troops approach the Frontier

KÚRBSKY. (*Galloping at their head.*) There, there it is;
    there is the Russian frontier!
    Fatherland! Holy Russia! I am thine!
    With scorn from off my clothing now I shake
    The foreign dust, and greedily I drink
    New air; it is my native air. O father,
    Thy soul hath now been solaced; in the grave
    Thy bones, disgraced, thrill with a sudden joy!
    Again doth flash our old ancestral sword,
    This glorious sword—the dread of dark Kazán!
    This good sword—servant of the tsars of Moscow!
    Now will it revel in its feast of slaughter,
    Serving the master of its hopes.

PRETENDER. (*Moves quietly with bowed head.*) How happy
    Is he, how flushed with gladness and with glory
    His stainless soul! Brave knight, I envy thee!
    The son of Kúrbsky, nurtured in exile,

Forgetting all the wrongs borne by thy father,
Redeeming his transgression in the grave,
Ready art thou for the son of great Iván
To shed thy blood, to give the fatherland
Its lawful tsar.   Righteous art thou ; thy soul
Should flame with joy.

KÚRBSKY.   And dost not thou likewise
Rejoice in spirit ?   There lies our Russia ; she
Is thine, tsarévich !   There thy people's hearts
Are waiting for thee, there thy Moscow waits,
Thy Kremlin, thy dominion.

PRETENDER.   Russian blood,
O Kúrbsky, first mus flow !   Thou for the tsar
Hast drawn the sword, thou art stainless ; but I lead you
Against your brothers ; I am summoning
Lithuania against Russia ; I am showing
To foes the longed-for way to beauteous Moscow !
But let my sin fall not on me, but thee,
Borís, the regicide !   Forward !   Set on !

KÚRBSKY.   Forward !   Advance !   And woe to Godunóv.
                    (*They gallop.   The troops cross the frontier.*)

THE COUNCIL OF THE TSAR

The TSAR, the PATRIARCH and Boyârs

TSAR. Is it possible ?   An unfrocked monk against us
　　　Leads rascal troops, a truant friar dares write
　　　Threats to us !   Then 'tis time to tame the madman !
　　　Trúbetskoy, set thou forth, and thou Basmánov ;
　　　My zealous governors need help.   Chernígov
　　　Already by the rebel is besieged ;
　　　Rescue the city and citizens.

BASMÁNOV.　　　　　　　　Three months
　　　Shall not pass, Sire, ere even rumour's tongue
　　　Shall cease to speak of the pretender ; caged
　　　In iron, like a wild beast from oversea,
　　　We'll hale him into Moscow, I swear by God.
　　　　　　　　　　　　(*Exit with* TRÚBETSKOY.`

TSAR. The Lord of Sweden hath by envoys tendered
　　　Alliance to me.   But we have no need
　　　To lean on foreign aid ; we have enough
　　　Of our own warlike people to repel
　　　Traitors and Poles.   I have refused.—Shchelkálov !

In every district to the governors
Send edicts, that they mount their steeds, and send
The people as of old on service ; likewise
Ride to the monasteries, and there enlist
The servants of the churchmen. In days of old,
When danger faced our country, hermits freely
Went into battle ; it is not now our wish
To trouble them ; no, let them pray for us ;
Such is the tsar's decree, such the resolve
Of his boyárs. And now a weighty question
We shall determine ; ye know how everywhere
The insolent pretender hath spread abroad
His artful rumours ; letters everywhere,
By him distributed, have sowed alarm
And doubt ; seditious whispers to and fro
Pass in the market-places ; minds are seething
We needs must cool them ; gladly would I refrain
From executions, but by what means and how ?
That we will now determine. Holy father,
Thou first declare thy thought.

PATRIARCH.   The Blessed One,
The All-Highest, hath instilled into thy soul,
Great lord, the spirit of kindness and meek patience ;
Thou wishest not perdition for the sinner,
Thou wilt wait quietly, until delusion

Shall pass away ; for pass away it will,
And truth's eternal sun will dawn on all.
Thy faithful bedesman, one in worldly matters
No prudent judge, ventures to-day to offer
His voice to thee. This offspring of the devil,
This unfrocked monk, has known how to appear
Dimítry to the people. Shamelessly
He clothed himself with the name of the tsarévich
As with a stolen vestment. It only needs
To tear it off—and he'll be put to shame
By his own nakedness. The means thereto
God hath Himself supplied. Know, sire, six years
Since then have fled ; 'twas in that very yea
When to the seat of sovereignty the Lord
Anointed thee—there came to me one evening
A simple shepherd, a venerable old man,
Who told me a strange secret. " In my young days,"
He said, " I lost my sight, and thenceforth knew not
Nor day, nor night, till my old age ; in vain
I plied myself with herbs and secret spells ;
In vain did I resort in adoration
To the great wonder-workers in the cloister ;
Bathed my dark eyes in vain with healing water
From out the holy wells. The Lord vouchsafed not
Healing to me. Then lost I hope at last,
And grew accustomed to my darkness. Even

Slumber showed not to me things visible,
Only of sounds I dreamed.   Once in deep sleep
I hear a childish voice ; it speaks to me :
' Arise, grandfather, go to Úglich town,
To the Cathedral of Transfiguration ;
There pray over my grave.   The Lord is gracious—
And I shall pardon thee.'   ' But who art thou ? '
I asked the childish voice.   ' I am the tsarévich
Dimítry, whom the Heavenly Tsar hath taken
Into His angel band, and I am now
A mighty wonder-worker.   Go, old man.'
I woke, and pondered.   What is this ?   Maybe
God will in very deed vouchsafe to me
Belated healing.   I will go.   I bent
My footsteps to the distant road.   I reached
Úglich, repair unto the holy minster,
Hear mass, and, glowing with zealous soul, I weep
Sweetly, as if the blindness from mine eyes
Were flowing out in tears.   And when the people
Began to leave, to my grandson I said :
' Lead me, Iván, to the grave of the tsarévich
Dimítry.'   The boy led me—and I scarce
Had shaped before the grave a silent prayer,
When sight illumed my eyeballs ; I beheld
The light of God, my grandson, and the tomb."
That is the tale, Sire, which the old man told.

(General agitation.   In the course of this speech Borís
several times wipes his face with his handkerchief.)

To Úglich then I sent, where it was learned
That many sufferers had found likewise
Deliverance at the grave of the tsarévich.
This is my counsel ; to the Kremlin send
The sacred relics, place them in the Cathedral
Of the Archangel ; clearly will the people
See then the godless vi'lain's fraud ; the might
Of the fiends will vanish as a cloud of dust.

(Silence.)

PRINCE SHUISKY. What mortal, holy father, knoweth the
    ways
Of the All-Highest ?   'Tis not for me to judge Him.
Untainted sleep and power of wonder-working
He may upon the child's remains bestow ;
But vulgar rumour must dispassionately
And diligently be tested ; is it for us,
In stormy times of insurrection,
To weigh so great a matter ?   Will men not say
That insolently we made of sacred things
A worldly instrument ?   Even now the people
Sway senselessly this way and that, even now
There are enough already of loud rumours ;
This is no time to vex the people's minds

With aught so unexpected, grave, and strange.
I myself see 'tis needful to demolish
The rumour spread abroad by the unfrocked monk ;
But for this end other and simpler means
Will serve.   Therefore, when it shall please thee, Sire,
I will myself appear in public places,
I will persuade, exhort away this madness,
And will expose the vagabond's vile fraud.

Tsar.   So be it !   My lord Patriarch, I pray thee
Go with us to the palace, where to-day
I must converse with thee.

(Exeunt ; all the boyárs *follow them.)*

1st Boyár.   (*Sotto voce to another.*)   Didst mark how pale
Our sovereign turned, how from his face there poured
A mighty sweat ?

2nd Boyár.   I durst not, I confess,
Uplift mine eyes, nor breathe, nor even stir.

1st Boyár.   Prince Shuisky has pulled it through.   A
splendid fellow !

A PLAIN NEAR NOVGOROD SEVERSK

(DECEMBER 21ST, 1604)

A BATTLE

SOLDIERS. (*Run in disorder.*) Woe, woe! The Tsarévich! The Poles! There they are! There they are!
(Captains *enter* : MÁRZHERET *and* WALTHER ROZEN.)

MÁRZHERET. Whither, whither? Allons! Go back!

ONE OF THE FUGITIVES. You go back, if you like, cursèd infidel.

MÁRZHERET. Quoi, quoi?

ANOTHER. Kva! kva! You like, you frog from over the sea, to croak at the Russian tsarévich; but we—we are orthodox.

MÁRZHERET. Qu'est-ce a dire " orthodox "? Sacrés gueux, maudite canaille! Mordieu, mein Herr, j'enrage; on dirait que ca n'a pas de bras pour frapper, ca n'a que des jambes pour fuir.

ROZEN. Es ist Schande.

MÁRZHERET. Ventre-saint gris ! Je ne bouge plus d'un pas ;
puisque le vin est tiré, il faut le boire. Qu'en dites-vous,
mein Herr ?

ROZEN. Sie haben Recht.

MÁRZHERET. Tudieu, il y fait chaud ! Ce diable de " Pretender," comme ils l'appellent, est un bougre, qui a du
poil au col ?—Qu'en pensez-vous, mein Herr ?

ROZEN. Ja.

MÁRZHERET. Hé ! voyez donc, voyez donc ! L'action s'en-
gage sur les derrières de l'ennemi. Ce doit être le brave
Basmánov, qui aurait fait une sortie.

ROZEN. Ich glaube das.

(*Enter* Germans.)

MÁRZHERET. Ha, ha ! voici nos allemands. Messieurs !
Mein Herr, dites-leur donc de se raillier et, sacrebleu,
chargeons !

ROZEN. Sehr gut. Halt ! (*The* Germans *halt*.) Marsch !

THE GERMANS. (*They march*.) Hilf Gott !

(*Fight. The* Russians *flee again*.)

POLES.   Victory!   Victory!   Glory to the tsar Dimítry!

DIMÍTRY.   (*On horseback.*)   Cease fighting.   We have conquered.   Enough!   Spare Russian blood.   Cease
fighting.

OPEN SPACE IN FRONT OF THE CATHEDRAL IN MOSCOW

THE PEOPLE

ONE OF THE PEOPLE. Will the tsar soon come out of the cathedral ?

ANOTHER. The mass is ended ; now the Te Deum is going on.

THE FIRST. What ! have they already cursed him ?

THE SECOND. I stood in the porch and heard how the deacon cried out :—Grishka Otrepiev is anathema !

THE FIRST. Let him curse to his heart's content ; the tsarévich has nothing to do with the Otrepiev.

THE SECOND. But they are now singing mass for the repose of the soul of the tsarévich.

THE FIRST. What ? A mass for the dead sung for a living man ? They'll suffer for it, the godless wretches !

A THIRD. Hist! A sound. Is it not the tsar?

A FOURTH. No, it is the idiot.

> (*An* idiot *enters, in an iron cap, hung round with chains, surrounded by* boys.)

THE BOYS. Nick, Nick, iron nightcap! T-r-r-r-r——

OLD WOMAN. Let him be, you young devils. Innocent one, pray thou for me a sinner.

IDIOT. Give, give, give a penny.

OLD WOMAN. There is a penny for thee; remember me in thy prayers.

IDIOT. (*Seats himself on the ground and sings :*)

> The moon sails on,
> The kitten cries,
> Nick, arise,
> Pray to God.

> (*The* boys *surround him again.*

ONE OF THEM. How do you do, Nick? Why don't you take off your cap?

> (*Raps him on the iron cap.*)

How it rings!

IDIOT. But I have got a penny.

BOYS. That's not true ; now, show it.

> (*They snatch the penny and run away.*)

IDIOT. (*Weeps.*) They have taken my penny, they are hurting Nick

THE PEOPLE. The tsar, the tsar is coming !

> (*The* TSAR *comes out from the Cathedral ; a* boyár *in front of him scatters alms among the poor.* Boyárs.)

IDIOT. Borís, Borís ! The boys are hurting Nick.

TSAR. Give him alms ! What is he crying for ?

IDIOT. The boys are hurting me . . . Give orders to slay them, as thou slewest the little tsarévich.

BOYÁRS. Go away, fool ! Seize the fool !

TSAR. Leave him alone. Pray thou for me, Nick.

> *Exit.*)

IDIOT. (*To himself.*) No, no ! It is impossible to pray for tsar Herod ; the Mother of God forbids it.

SYEVSK

The PRETENDER, surrounded by his supporters

PRETENDER.   Where is the prisoner ?

A POLE.   Here.

PRETENDER.   Call him before me
                              (*A Russian* prisoner *enters.*)
    Who art thou ?

PRISONER.   Rozhnóv, a nobleman of Moscow.

PRETENDER.   Hast long been in the service ?

PRISONER.   About a month.

PRETENDER.   Art not ashamed, Rozhnôv, that thou hast
    drawn
    The sword against me ?

PRISONER.   What else could I do ?
    'Twas not our fault.

PRETENDER.   Didst fight beneath the walls
    Of Séversk ?

PRISONER.   'Twas two weeks after the battle
I came from Moscow.

PRETENDER,   What of Godunóv ?

PRISONER. The battle's loss, Mstislávsky's wound, hath
caused him
Much apprehension ; Shuisky he hath sent
To take command.

PRETENDER.   But why hath he recalled
Basmánov unto Moscow ?

PRISONER.   The tsar rewarded
His services with honour and with gold.
Basmánov in the council of the tsar
Now sits.

PRETENDER.   The army had more need of him.
Well, how go things in Moscow ?

PRISONER.   All is quiet,
Thank God.

PRETENDER.   Say, do they look for me ?

PRISONER.   God knows ;
   They dare not talk too much there now.   Of some
   The tongues have been cut off, of others even
   The heads.   It is a fearsome state of things—
   Each day an execution.   All the prisons
   Are crammed.   Wherever two or three forgather
   In public places, instantly a spy
   Worms himself in ; the tsar himself examines
   At leisure the denouncers.   It is just
   Sheer misery ; so silence is the best.

PRETENDER.   An enviable life for the tsar's people !
   Well, how about the army ?

PRISONER.   What of them ?
   Clothed and full-fed they are content with all.

PRETENDER.   But is there much of it ?

PRISONER.   God knows.

PRETENDER.   All told
   Will there be thirty thousand ?

PRISONER.   Yes ; 'twill run
   Even to fifty thousand.
        (*The Pretender reflects ; those around him glance at
        one another.*)

PRETENDER. Well! Of me
What say they in your camp ?

PRISONER. Your graciousness
They speak of ; say that thou, Sire, (be not wrath),
Art a thief, but a fine fellow.

PRETENDER. (*Laughing.*) Even so
I'll prove myself to them in deed. My friends,
We will not wait for Shuisky ; I wish you joy ;
To-morrow, battle.

(*Exit.*)

ALL. Long life to Dimítry !

A POLE. To-morrow, battle ! They are fifty thousand,
And we scarce fifteen thousand. He is mad !

ANOTHER. That's nothing, friend. A single Pole can
challenge
Five hundred Muscovites.

PRISONER. Yes, thou mayst challenge !
But when it comes to fighting, then, thou braggart,
Thou'lt run away.

POLE. If thou hadst had a sword,
Insolent prisoner, then (*pointing to his sword*) with this
I'ld soon
Have vanquished thee.

PRISONER. A Russian can make shift
Without a sword ; how like you this (*shows his fist*), you
fool ?

    (*The* Pole *looks at him haughtily and departs in
silence. All laugh.*)

A FOREST

PRETENDER and PÚSHKIN

(In the background lies a dying horse)

PRETENDER.   Ah, my poor horse !   How gallantly he charged
    To-day in the last battle, and when wounded,
    How swiftly bore me.   My poor horse !

PÚSHKIN.   (*To himself.*)   Well, here's
    A great ado about a horse, when all
    Our army's smashed to bits.

PRETENDER.   Listen ! Perhaps
    He's but exhausted by the loss of blood,
    And will recover.

PÚSHKIN.   Nay, nay ; he is dying.

PRETENDER.   (*Goes to his horse.*)
    My poor horse !—what to do ?   Take off the bridle,
    And loose the girth.   Let him at least die free.
        (*He unbridles and unsaddles the horse.   Some Poles
            enter.*)
    Good day to you, gentlemen !   How is't I see not

Kúrbsky among you ?   I did note to-day
How to the thick of the fight he clove his path ;
Around the hero's sword, like swaying ears
Of corn, hosts thronged ; but higher than all of them
His blade was brandished, and his terrible cry
Drowned all cries else.   Where is my knight ?

POLE.   He fell
On the field of battle.

PRETENDER.   Honour to the brave,
And peace be on his soul !   How few unscathed
Are left us from the fight !   Accursèd Cossacks,
Traitors and miscreants, you, you it is
Have ruined us !   Not even for three minutes
To keep the foe at bay !   I'll teach the villains !
Every tenth man I'll hang.   Brigands !

PÚSHKIN.   Whoe'er
Be guilty, all the same we were clean worsted,
Routed !

PRETENDER.   But yet we nearly conquered.   Just
When I had dealt with their front rank, the Germans
Repulsed us utterly.   But they're fine fellows !
By God ! fine fellows !   I love them for it.   From them
I'll form an honourable troop.

PÚSHKIN. And where
Shall we now spend the night ?

PRETENDER. Why, here, in the forest.
Why not this for our night quarters ? At daybreak
We'll take the road, and dine in Rilsk. Good-night.
(*He lies down, puts a saddle under his head, and falls
asleep.*)

PÚSHKIN. A pleasant sleep, tsarévich ! Smashed to bits,
Rescued by flight alone, he is as careless
As a simple child ; 'tis clear that Providence
Protects him, and we, my friends, will not lose heart.

MOSCOW. PALACE OF THE TSAR

BORÍS. BASMÁNOV

TSAR.   He is vanquished, but what profit lies in that?
We are crowned with a vain conquest; he has mustered
Again his scattered forces, and anew
Threatens us from the ramparts of Putívl.
Meanwhile what are our heroes doing?   They stand
At Krom, where from its rotten battlements
A band of Cossacks braves them.   There is glory!
No, I am ill content with them; thyself
I shall despatch to take command of them;
I give authority not to birth, but brains.
Their pride of precedence, let it be wounded!
The time has come for me to hold in scorn
The murmur of distinguished nobodies,
And quash pernicious custom.

BASMÁNOV.   Ay, my lord
Blessèd a hundredfold will be that day
When fire consumes the lists of noblemen
With their dissensions, their ancestral pride.

TSAR. That day is not far off ; let me but first
    Subdue the insurrection of the people.

BASMÁNOV. Why trouble about that ? The people always
    Are prone to secret treason ; even so
    The swift steed champs the bit ; so doth a lad
    Chafe at his father's ruling. But what then ?
    The rider quietly controls the steed,
    The father sways the son.

TSAR.   Sometimes the horse
    Doth throw the rider, nor is the son at all times
    Quite 'neath the father's will ; we can restrain
    The people only by unsleeping sternness.
    So thought Iván, sagacious autocrat
    And storm-subduer ; so his fierce grandson thought.
    No, no, kindness is lost upon the people ;
    Act well—it thanks you not at all ; extort
    And execute—'twill be no worse for you.

                          (*Enter a* boyár.,
What now ?

BOYÁR.   The foreign guests are come.

TSAR.   I go
    To welcome them. Basmánov, wait, stay here ;
    I still have need to speak a word with thee.

                                (*Exit.*)

BASMÁNOV. High sovereign spirit! God grant he may
  subdue
  The accurst Otrepiev; and much, still much
  Of good he'll do for Russia. A great thought
  Within his mind has taken birth; it must not
  Be suffered to grow cold. What a career
  For me when the ancestral horn he breaks
  Of the nobility. I have no rivals
  In war. I shall stand closest to the throne—
  And it may chance— But what is that strange
  sound?

>   (*Alarum.* Boyárs *and* court-attendants *run in
>   disorder, meet each other and whisper.*)

ONE. Fetch a physician!

ANOTHER.   Quickly to the Patriarch!

A THIRD. He calls for the tsarévich, the tsarévich!

A FOURTH. A confessor!

BASMÁNOV.   What has happened?

A FIFTH AND SIXTH.   The tsar is ill,
  The tsar is dying.

BASMÁNOV.   Good God!

A FIFTH.   Upon the throne
   He sat, and suddenly he fell ; blood gushed
   From his mouth and ears.

   (*The* TSAR *is carried in on a chair.   All the Tsar's
        household ; all the* boyárs.)

TSAR.   Let all depart—alone
   Leave the tsarévich with me. (*All withdraw.*) I am dying ;
   Let us embrace.   Farewell, my son ; this hour
   Thou wilt begin to reign.—O God, my God !
   This hour I shall appear before Thy presence—
   And have no time to purge my soul with shrift.
   But yet, my son, I feel thou art dearer to me
   Than is my soul's salvation—be it so !
   A subject was I born ; it seemed ordained
   That I should die a subject in obscurity.
   Yet I attained to sovereignty ; but how ?
   Ask not.   Enough that thou art innocent.
   In justice now thou'lt reign ; and I alone
   Am answerable for all to God.   Dear son,
   Cherish no false delusion, of thy free will
   Blind not thyself.   Stormy the days wherein
   Thou dost assume the crown.   He is dangerous,
   This strange pretender ; with a fearful name
   He is armed.   For many a year experienced

In rule, I could restrain revolt and treason;
They quaked with fear before me; treachery
Dared not to raise its voice; but thou, a boy,
An inexperienced ruler, how wilt thou
Govern amid the tempests, quench revolt,
Shackle sedition? But God is great! He gives
Wisdom to youth, to weakness strength.—Give ear;
Firstly, select a steadfast counsellor,
Of cool, ripe years, loved of the people, honoured
Mid the boyárs for birth and fame—even Shuisky.
The army craves to-day a skilful leader;
Basmánov send, and firmly bear the murmurs
Of the boyárs. Thou from thy early years
Didst sit with me in council, thou dost know
The formal course of government; change not
Procedure. Custom is the soul of states.
Of late I have been forced to reinstate
Bans, executions—these thou canst rescind;
And they will bless thee, as they blessed thy uncle
When he obtained the throne of the Terrible.
At the same time, little by little, tighten
Anew the reins of government; now slacken;
But let them not slip from thy hands. Be gracious,
Accessible to foreigners, accept
Their service trustfully. Preserve with strictness
The Church's discipline. Be taciturn;

H

The royal voice must never lose itself
Upon the air in emptiness, but like
A sacred bell must sound but to announce
Some great disaster or great festival.
Dear son, thou art approaching to those years
When woman's beauty agitates our blood.
Preserve, preserve the sacred purity
Of innocence and proud shamefacedness ;
He, who through passion has been wont to wallow
In vicious pleasures in his youthful days,
Becomes in manhood bloodthirsty and surly ;
His mind untimely darkens. Of thy household
Be always head ; show honour to thy mother,
But rule thy house thyself ; thou art a man
And tsar to boot. Be loving to thy sister—
Thou wilt be left of her the sole protector.

FEÓDOR. (*On his knees.*) No, no ; live on, my father, and
reign long ;
Without thee both the folk and we will perish.

TSAR. All is at end for me—mine eyes grow dark,
I feel the coldness of the grave——

> (*Enter the* PATRIARCH *and* prelates ; *behind them all
> the* boyárs *lead the* TSARÍTSA *by the hand* ; *the*
> TSARÉVNA *is sobbing.*)

Who's there ?

Ah, 'tis the vestment—so ! the holy tonsure—
The hour has struck.   The tsar becomes a monk,
And the dark sepulchre will be my cell.
Wait yet a little, my lord Patriarch,
I still am tsar.   Listen to me, boyárs :
To this my son I now commit the tsardom ;
Do homage to Feódor.   Basmánov, thou,
And ye, my friends, on the grave's brink I pray you
To serve my son with zeal and rectitude !
As yet he is both young and uncorrupted.
Swear ye ?

BOYÁRS.   We swear.

TSAR.   I am content.   Forgive me
Both my temptations and my sins, my wilful
And secret injuries.—Now, holy father,
Approach thou ; I am ready for the rite.

> (*The rite of the tonsure begins.   The women are
> carried out swooning.*)

A TENT

BASMÁNOV leads in PUSHKIN

BASMÁNOV. Here enter, and speak freely. So to me
He sent thee.

PÚSHKIN.   He doth offer thee his friendship
And the next place to his in the realm of Moscow.

BASMÁNOV. But even thus highly by Feódor am I
Already raised ; the army I command ;
For me he scorned nobility of rank
And the wrath of the boyárs. I have sworn to him
Allegiance.

PÚSHKIN.   To the throne's lawful successor
Allegiance thou hast sworn ; but what if one
More lawful still be living ?

BASMÁNOV.   Listen, Púshkin :
Enough of that ; tell me no idle tales !
I know the man.

Púshkin.   Russia and Lithuania
Have long acknowledged him to be Dimítry ;
But, for the rest, I do not vouch for it.
Perchance he is indeed the real Dimítry ;
Perchance but a pretender ; only this
I know, that soon or late the son of Borís
Will yield Moscow to him.

Basmánov.   So long as I
Stand by the youthful tsar, so long he will not
Forsake the throne.   We have enough of troops,
Thank God !   With victory I will inspire them,
And whom will you against me send, the Cossack
Karél or Mníshek ?   Are your numbers many ?
In all, eight thousand.

Púshkin.   You mistake ; they will not
Amount even to that.   I say myself
Our army is mere trash, the Cossacks only
Rob villages, the Poles but brag and drink ;
The Russians—what shall I say ?—with you I'll not
Dissemble ; but, Basmánov, dost thou know
Wherein our strength lies ?   Not in the army, no,
Nor Polish aid, but in opinion—yes,
In popular opinion.   Dost remember
The triumph of Dimítry, dost remember

His peaceful conquests, when, without a blow
The docile towns surrendered, and the mob
Bound the recalcitrant leaders ?   Thou thyself
Saw'st it ; was it of their free-will our troops
Fought with him ?   And when did they so ?   Borís
Was then supreme.   But would they now ?—Nay, nay,
It is too late to blow on the cold embers
Of this dispute ; with all thy wits and firmness
Thou'lt not withstand him.   Were't not better for thee
To furnish to our chief a wise example,
Proclaim Dimítry tsar, and by that act
Bind him your friend for ever ?   How thinkest thou ?

BASMÁNOV.   To-morrow thou shalt know.

PÚSHKIN.   Resolve.

BASMÁNOV.   Farewell.

PÚSHKIN.   Ponder it well, Basmánov.

                                          (*Exit.*)

BASMÁNOV.   He is right.
Everywhere treason ripens ; what shall I do ?
Wait, that the rebels may deliver me
In bonds to the Otrepiev ?   Had I not better
Forestall the stormy onset of the flood,
Myself to—ah ! but to forswear mine oath !

Dishonour to deserve from age to age !
The trust of my young sovereign to requite
With horrible betrayal !   'Tis a light thing
For a disgraced exile to meditate
Sedition and conspiracy ; but I ?
Is it for me, the favourite of my lord ?—
But death—but power—the people's miseries . . .

(He ponders.)

Here ! Who is   there ? *(Whistles.)*   A horse here :
  Sound the muster !

PUBLIC SQUARE IN MOSCOW

PÚSHKIN enters, surrounded by the people

THE PEOPLE. The tsarévich a boyár hath sent to us.
Let's hear what the boyár will tell us. Hither !
Hither !

PÚSHKIN. (*On a platform.*) Townsmen of Moscow ! The
tsarévich
Bids me convey his greetings to you. (*He bows.*) Ye
know
How Divine Providence saved the tsarévich
From out the murderer's hands ; he went to punish
His murderer, but God's judgment hath already
Struck down Borís. All Russia hath submitted
Unto Dimítry ; with heartfelt repentance
Basmánov hath himself led forth his troops
To swear allegiance to him. In love, in peace
Dimítry comes to you. Would ye, to please
The house of Godunóv, uplift a hand
Against the lawful tsar, against the grandson
Of Monomakh ?

THE PEOPLE.   Not we.

PÚSHKIN.   Townsmen of Moscow !
    The world well knows how much ye have endured
    Under the rule of the cruel stranger ; ban,
    Dishonour, executions, taxes, hardships,
    Hunger—all these ye have experienced.
    Dimítry is disposed to show you favour,
    Courtiers, boyárs, state-servants, soldiers, strangers,
    Merchants—and every honest man.   Will ye
    Be stubborn without reason, and in pride
    Flee from his kindness ?   But he himself is coming
    To his ancestral throne with dreadful escort.
    Provoke not ye the tsar to wrath, fear God,
    And swear allegiance to the lawful ruler ;
    Humble yourselves ; forthwith send to Dimítry
    The Metropolitan, deacons, boyárs,
    And chosen men, that they may homage do
    To their lord and father.

                    (*Exit.   Clamour of the* People.)

THE PEOPLE.   What is to be said ?
    The boyár spake truth.   Long live Dimítry, our father !

A PEASANT ON THE PLATFORM. People! To the Kremlin!
  To the Royal palace!
  The whelp of Borís go bind!

THE PEOPLE. (*Rushing in a crowd.*)

                                Bind, drown him! Hail
  Dimítry! Perish the race of Godunóv!

THE KREMLIN. HOUSE OF BORÍS

A GUARD on the Staircase. FEÓDOR at a Window

BEGGAR. Give alms, for Christ's sake

GUARD. Go away; it is forbidden to speak to the prisoners.

FEÓDOR. Go, old man, I am poorer than thou; thou art at liberty.

> (KSENIA, *veiled, also comes to the window.*)

ONE OF THE PEOPLE. Brother and sister—poor children, like birds in a cage.

SECOND PERSON. Are you going to pity them? Accursèd family!

FIRST PERSON. The father was a villain, but the children are innocent.

SECOND PERSON. The apple does not fall far from the apple-tree.

KSENIA. Dear brother! dear brother! I think the boyárs are coming to us.

FEÓDOR. That is Golitsin, Mosalsky. I do not know the others.

KSENIA. Ah! dear brother, my heart sinks.
(GOLITSIN, MOSALSKY, MOLCHANOV, *and* SHEREFEDINOV; *behind them three archers.*)

THE PEOPLE. Make way, make way; the boyárs come.
(*They enter the house.*)

ONE OF THE PEOPLE. What have they come for?

SECOND. Most like to make Feódor Godunóv take the oath.

THIRD. Very like. Hark! what a noise in the house! What an uproar! They are fighting!

THE PEOPLE. Do you hear? A scream! That was a woman's voice. We will go up. We will go up!—The doors are fastened—the cries cease—the noise continues.
(*The doors are thrown open.* MOSALSKY *appears on the staircase.*)

MOSALSKY. People! Maria Godunóv and her son Feódor have poisoned themselves. We have seen their dead bodies.

(The People are silent with horror.)

Why are ye silent? Cry, Long live the tsar Dimítry Ivánovich!

(The People are speechless.)

THE END